THOROUGHBRED

W9-ATJ-019

CHRISTINA'S SHINING STAR

CREATED BY
JOANNA CAMPBELL

WRITTEN BY
MARY ANDERSON

HarperEntertainment
An Imprint of HarperCollinsPublishers

HarperEntertainment
An Imprint of HarperCollins*Publishers*
10 East 53rd Street, New York, NY 10022-5299

Produced by 17th Street Productions,
an Alloy Online, Inc., company

HarperCollins books are available at special quantity discounts for bulk
purchases for sales promotions, premiums, or fund-raising.
For information please call or write:
Special Markets Department, HarperCollins Publishers Inc.,
10 East 53rd Street, New York, NY 10022-5299.
Telephone: (212) 207-7528. Fax: (212) 207-7222.

ISBN 0-06-009050-2

First printing: April 2003

Printed in the United States of America

Visit HarperEntertainment on the World Wide Web at
www.harpercollins.com

❖ 10 9 8 7 6 5 4 3 2 1

To my dear friend Andrea Jackson and
her movie star horse, Captain

CHRISTINA'S
SHINING STAR

CHRISTINA REESE KEPT HER EYES FOCUSED BETWEEN Wonder's Star's flattened ears, searching the wall of galloping horses in front of her chestnut colt for an opening. But there were no gaps between any of the Thoroughbreds blocking them. Star and seventeen-year-old Christina, racing in Whitebrook Farm's blue-and-white silks, would never be able to charge down the final stretch of the Churchill Downs racetrack to win the Kentucky Derby.

A clod of dirt, flung up by one of the colts in front of them, broke against Christina's cheek. She barely noticed the sting, she was so focused on finding a way to maneuver into the clear. Beneath her, she felt her three-year-old colt's powerful muscles quiver with tension. Star hated to be boxed in. He strained against the hold she had on his reins, pumping his head against the pressure as he tried to break loose. Christina knew that if he was given his head, Star would run right over the horses blocking their way.

Christina shot a glance to her left, but Vicky Frontiere, mounted on TV Time, was trying to push her colt around War Ghost, Derry O'Dell, and Ingleside, the horses in front of Star. Christina groaned to herself. Vicky was a top-notch jockey, and by the determined expression on her face, Christina knew that she was trying to give TV Time a fighting chance to pull off a win. Which meant Vicky wasn't going to fall back, giving Star room to go wide and get out of the trap. But Christina could tell by the effort TV Time was putting into each stride that the colt didn't have the staying power to move ahead of the other horses.

Christina had been so sure that Star's start from the number three position would put them in a good place right at the beginning of the race, she hadn't thought beyond it. She hadn't anticipated Perfect Image, Gratis, and Speed.com getting into a speed duel right from the start. *All I could think about was the fact that I'm actually racing Star in the Kentucky Derby. What am I going to do?* she berated herself, searching intently for a way to move Star ahead.

From the announcer's voice, blaring over the loud-speakers, Christina knew the focus of the race was on Image, the black filly Christina's cousin, Melanie Graham, was riding. Christina listened to the race happening among Image, Gratis, and Speed.com. As the only filly running in the field of nine, Image had been the focus of the media's coverage of the race for weeks before Derby day. Now, with her tremendous effort to keep in front of the field, Image and the two horses who challenged her had everyone's full attention. The other six horses on the track didn't seem to exist.

Derry O'Dell swerved slightly, and through the minute gap, Christina caught a glimpse of Celtic Mist's rump. The gray colt was running strongly. Emilio Casados, in Townsend Acres' green-and-gold colors, was bringing his whip down on Celtic Mist's left hip. The colt surged forward, narrowing the lead between his mount and Melanie's black filly. Image was flanked by Speed.com, the colt trained by Alexis Huffman, and Gratis, the massive bay colt owned by Ben al-Rihani of Tall Oaks Farm.

Christina started to urge Star forward, but the opening made by Derry O'Dell's move wasn't big enough for them to slip into a better position. Beneath her, Star's snorted breaths expressed his own frustration and stress. Christina felt worry grip her. Highstrung and delicate, a racehorse could be devastated by stress. Star had overcome incredible setbacks to make it into the Derby, and she knew he wanted to win the race as much as she did.

She gave her head a quick snap to clear her thoughts, then leaned forward over the colt's neck. "Come on," she muttered, searching desperately for a chance to get Star away from the crowd. She knew that if he was free to move out, Star could tear a hole in the wind and sweep past the lead horses to cross the finish line first. But as they bore down on the finish line, Star was dead last, and there was nothing she could do to change that.

Christina heard the combined voices of the crowd swell into a roar of excitement. "Perfect Image wins the Kentucky Derby!" the announcer cried.

So Melanie had pulled it off! Christina felt a rush of pride in her cousin's accomplishment, but that feeling was tinged with disappointment over the fact that the race was over and Star had never even reached his full speed. Christina began to pull him up as they reached the finish line, reminding herself that anything could happen in a horse race.

Suddenly the sounds from the grandstand turned from yells of excitement to cries of dismay. Ahead of Star, horses were swerving left and right, avoiding something on the track. Christina automatically steered Star to the right, then glanced down to see what had caused the commotion.

A gasp of horror caught in her throat as she spotted Image lying on the track. Melanie, her green-and-white silks streaked with dirt, was scrambling to her feet and darting back to her fallen filly.

Christina brought Star up as quickly as she could. The colt was lathered and breathing heavily, but she knew it wasn't from a hard race. It was from the pent-up energy of not being able to run. She slipped from his back as Dani Martens met her on the track. The handler quickly clipped a lead onto Star's bridle as Christina pressed a hand against his side, feeling his heart pounding against his ribs.

"Image went down just over the finish line," Dani explained in a rush, gripping the lead as Star pranced and tossed his head, dancing in circles around her. "I'll take care of Star for you so you can help Melanie." She patted the colt's lathered neck. "Easy, boy," Dani crooned softly. "It's time to settle down now."

Christina hesitated for a moment, her attention still on Star. The colt was upset, but she knew Dani would get him calmed down. She needed to see if there was anything she could do for Melanie and Image.

"He needs a lot of walking out," Christina told

Dani, resting her hand on the colt's damp neck.

Dani nodded in understanding, her eyes on Star as the colt flung his head up, trying to tear the lead line from her hands. "I'll take care of him, Chris," she promised, turning Star toward the track's backside. "You go take care of Melanie." As Dani led the antsy colt away, Christina hurried to the terrible scene near the finish line.

By the time she reached Melanie and Image, the track crew had set up large screens to keep the spectators from seeing the injured horse. The sight of the filly writhing in pain was upsetting, and the attending veterinarian needed to concentrate on helping the horse without the distraction of the concerned fans. People were crowded against the rail, trying to see what was happening behind the barriers, calling out questions to Christina as she started around one of the screens. Melanie was lying across Image's neck. The filly's left front cannon jutted off at an awkward angle, and a wave of nausea swept over Christina at the sight of Image's broken leg. She started forward, ready to put her arms around her cousin. She needed to get Melanie away from Image so that the track veterinarian could euthanize the filly. But as she took a step, a hand suddenly gripped her shoulder.

"You'll need to stay out of the way," a voice commanded. Christina turned to see a track attendant frowning at her.

"But I'm—" Christina started to protest.

"Excuse me," another voice broke in. "This is the filly's owner." Christina glanced over to see a track official escorting Jazz, the young rock musician who owned Image, into the area. Jazz didn't seem aware of Christina. His worried gaze was on Melanie and his badly injured racehorse.

"Go right ahead, sir," the attendant said, still holding Christina back. "You'll need to leave," he told her, then stepped between Christina and the fallen filly, blocking her from getting closer to her cousin.

Christina hesitated for a second, then turned and walked down the middle of the track, avoiding the curious crowd that was clustered along the rail. Melanie didn't need her there. She had Jazz to take care of things. Melanie's father, Will Graham, and his wife, Susan, had flown down from New York to watch the race. Christina was sure they would be brought onto the track, too. Melanie would have plenty of people there for her.

When Christina slipped through the gate near the stabling area, she saw several reporters between her and the barns. Before any of them noticed her, Christina ducked around the side of a building and hurried along the shadowy length, relieved that she had managed to avoid any questions about Image or about Star's performance. But when she came around the corner of the building, the dead box loomed in front of her.

Christina stopped abruptly and stared at the large container, which was used to hold the remains of horses who had to be destroyed at the track. The box was empty at the moment, but a vision of Image lying on the track in severe pain filled Christina's mind. She saw the filly clearly, her leg sticking out as the veterinarian leaned over her, Melanie across her neck in her dirt-spattered silks.

Another wave of sickness caught Christina, and she slumped against the side of the building, propping her hands on her knees. She closed her eyes, forcing herself to breathe slowly, trying to will the terrible picture from her mind. She stayed there for several minutes, knowing she needed to get out of her silks and help Dani with Star, but she couldn't bring herself to move. The sounds from the track faded into the distance as she hid in the quiet shadows behind the back of the shed rows.

"Hey, I wondered where you'd gone off to."

Christina straightened quickly and looked up at tall, dark-haired Parker Townsend. Parker had taken time out from his busy schedule as a member of the United States Equestrian Team to watch the Kentucky Derby. Parker's parents, Brad and Lavinia Townsend, had a private box for watching the action, but Parker had made it a point to be at the rail for the start of the race. She knew he had shown up more for her and Star than to watch his parents' colt, Celtic Mist. "Did you see what happened to Image?" she asked softly. "What a nightmare for Melanie and Jazz."

Parker nodded grimly. "Her leg snapped just as she got over the finish line," he said. "But Image won the race, Chris." He smiled weakly. "Melanie and Image won the Kentucky Derby. Not too many fillies have done that."

Knowing what Melanie and Image had accomplished made Christina feel a little better. She and Star might have finished last, but Melanie and Image had given the fans an unforgettable race. "At least Melanie will have that to remember," she said sadly. She couldn't imagine how her cousin would deal with having Image destroyed.

Parker put his hand on Christina's shoulder and gave it a gentle squeeze. "They haven't made a decision about Image yet," he said. "Mel's quick thinking, keeping the filly down and not letting her do any more damage to that leg, may have saved her life."

"Good," was all Christina could murmur. The weight of Parker's hand on her shoulder made her feel weak, and she fought back the urge to throw herself into his arms and burst into tears.

"Are you all right?" Parker asked, frowning at her. "You look a little pale. You and Star really got into a bad spot on the track. What went wrong?"

"I'm fine," she said, squaring her shoulders. She wasn't going to break down and cry over losing the race. "How did Celtic Mist place?" she asked.

Brad Townsend had been so sure of his colt that he had opened Townsend Acres' facilities to Melanie and Image when the pre-Derby publicity had been too much for Whitebrook to manage. After all his bragging and confident talk about Celtic Mist's ability, Brad must have been livid when Image crossed the finish line first.

Parker rolled his eyes. "Dad's precious colt came in second."

"I'll bet he wasn't too happy about that," Christina said. A half smile twisted her mouth as she thought of Brad trying to control himself when the press was shoving microphones in his face.

"That's an understatement." Parker made a sound that was somewhere between a dry laugh and a snort of disgust. "I didn't stick around to hear what he had to say," he admitted. "But you know perfectly well that second isn't nearly good enough for a Townsend Acres horse." Then he started to grin. "Ben and Cindy are ecstatic, though. Gratis took third."

"That's great," Christina said. She was sure Wolf, the young jockey Cindy McLean had hired, was thrilled.

"I was pretty worried about you and Star," Parker said, eyeing her closely. "I could barely see you, stuck in the back. How did that happen? It looked like Star came out of the gate ready to tear up the track."

"He did. It wasn't exactly our shining moment." Christina grimaced. "I'd better go check on Star," she added, wishing Parker would get the hint that she didn't want to discuss the fact that not only had Star not finished in the top three, but the colt had finished last.

"I went by the Whitebrook stalls when I was looking for you," Parker said. "Dani has Star between the shed rows, still walking him out." He eyed the dead box and turned his back to the grisly reminder of one of racing's terrible realities. "I think the stable would be a much more pleasant place to hang around than back here."

Christina glanced at the box again and shuddered. "You are absolutely right," she said. Parker draped his arm over her shoulders, and they left the area, heading for the rows of stalls to find Dani and Star.

• • •

11

A little over a week later, Christina stood outside the yearling barn at Whitebrook, her parents' Thoroughbred breeding and training farm located near Lexington, Kentucky. Mike Reese and Ashleigh Griffen had worked hard to build up their farm. With the main house, the caretaker's cottage, and three sprawling barns, Whitebrook was small compared to some of the huge, corporate-owned facilities in the area. But Christina thought Whitebrook was the best farm in Kentucky. Unlike the owners of some of the larger farms, the Reeses worked closely with each of their beloved animals.

Christina had been spending a lot of time at Townsend Acres while Melanie settled in at the guest cottage there, recovering from her own injuries after Image broke down during the Derby.

While she had been in the hospital being treated for a broken rib, Melanie had been despondent, thinking Image would have to be destroyed. But Brad Townsend had come through, much to everyone's surprise. Christina had been elated to hear that after surgery to repair her broken leg, Image was going to go through therapy at the Townsends' medical facility. The filly's prognosis was good, and now Christina was eager to get back to the routine of life at Whitebrook. The Townsends had an impressive setup, but she couldn't imagine being happy living there. Brad and Lavinia Townsend, Parker's parents, certainly didn't seem content with what they had.

Christina gazed across the sweeping bluegrass pastures that surrounded the white-painted barns and the knoll where the Reeses' old white farmhouse sat. It was the only home Christina had ever known, and normally she enjoyed the peaceful setting. But at the moment Whitebrook seemed almost *too* quiet. The pre-Derby frenzy was past. Reporters no longer crowded the driveway, waiting for a glimpse of Star or Image. The phones had stopped ringing constantly with people trying to get interviews with Whitebrook staff. Much of the interest in the farm had faded when Image had been moved to Townsend Acres before the Derby. Now, with Star's humiliating loss in the race, the farm might as well have fallen off the planet.

Christina gave a defiant shrug. It didn't matter to her, she thought. If Star had been in the clear, the race surely would have ended differently.

She glanced toward Star's turnout, where the colt was grazing quietly. Keeping the Thoroughbreds confined after a race was an important precaution. Highstrung and still eager to run after gearing up for weeks to run for only a few minutes, the horses were never let loose in a large field upon returning to the farm. Without a jockey to control him, an overwrought Thoroughbred could easily injure himself. So for a few days after the Derby, Star had been limited to the paddock near his stall.

Christina sighed to herself. Considering that Star hadn't had the slightest chance to run his best, she wouldn't have been surprised if he started galloping madly even in the tiny enclosure. In fact, she almost wished he would show some desire to break loose and gallop all out. Instead, the chestnut Thoroughbred seemed almost too calm, and that worried Christina.

Since the disastrous Derby he had been on layoff. Her parents were taking Will and Susan Graham to the airport so that they could fly back to their home and jobs in New York. The next day Star would resume his training schedule to gear up for the Preakness, the second of the Triple Crown races. And Christina was determined that the upcoming race would be one with a happy ending for both of them.

Behind her in the yearling barn, Christina could hear Ian McLean, Whitebrook's head trainer, talking with Maureen Mack, his assistant, about the new yearling crop. Christina's thoughts strayed to the half-dozen yearlings Whitebrook was prepping for next year. She thought of Miss America's bay colt, Royal Blue, wondering if the Blues King foal might be her next chance

14

for a Triple Crown win. She quickly dashed the idea away, feeling as though she was being untrue to Star by thinking ahead that way. They still had the Preakness and the Belmont to run, and she knew Star had it in him to win the prestigious competitions if she could guide him through the races competently.

She hurried across the barnyard and let herself into Star's paddock. The colt raised his head and nickered softly, then crossed the grassy enclosure to meet her.

"You *do* have it in you to win, don't you?" she asked, gazing into the colt's dark eyes. She searched his expression for any sign of depression or stress, but Star looked back steadily, his eyes clear and bright. "We'll be able to do it," she said aloud, reassuring herself more than the colt. "We learned from the Derby, didn't we?"

Star snorted softly and bobbed his head, nudging at her as he searched her pockets for a treat.

"No goodies," she said, gently pushing his nose away. "Tomorrow we get back into training mode. Your little rest is over—it's time to get back to work. In a couple of weeks we'll be back at the track. And this time," she said, cupping Star's jaw in her hands and looking at him with a mock frown, "we're going to come out of the gate in first place and stay there the whole way, right?"

Star tossed his head and pulled away from her. He took a few steps across the pasture before he dropped his nose to nibble at the grass underfoot.

Christina exhaled heavily and bit at her lower lip. She was sure Star still had the spirit of a winner, but a deeper, more nagging question burned at her, leaving her feeling unsettled.

Star might have it in him to win. But did she?

2

THE SUN WAS BARELY OVER THE HORIZON ON THURSDAY morning when Christina brought Star to a stop near a gap in the rail of Whitebrook's half-mile practice track. Ashleigh scribbled a couple of notes on the clipboard she held before looking up at Christina. "Star's looking great," she said. "I still don't understand how you managed to get trapped at the Derby."

Christina slipped from Star's saddle and unbuckled the girth as Ashleigh took hold of his reins. The colt was sweating after his work, and steam rose from his damp coat. "You watched the video of the race at least a dozen times," Christina said, throwing a cooling sheet over Star's back. "If you saw anything useful, I'm sure

17

you would have told me." She busied herself buckling the blanket into place to avoid looking at her mother.

"That's the problem," Ashleigh said, giving the colt's neck a pet. "I couldn't see any reason why that should have happened."

Christina started to speak. It would be so easy to blame the loss on a lot of things, but instead she pinched her mouth shut. She knew her mother didn't want excuses, and Christina really didn't have any. Bad luck, bad riding, bad timing—whatever it was, she and Star had lost, and that was all that mattered.

"We can discuss this later," Ashleigh said. "You need to walk Star out, and I need to go talk to Naomi and Maureen about this weekend's race schedule at Churchill Downs."

"Do you have any races planned for me this weekend?" Christina asked, taking Star's lead line.

Ashleigh shook her head. "No, I want you to continue to work with Star. You need to keep your focus on the Preakness."

Christina released a sigh and walked Star away. She knew she needed to get her mind off the Derby loss and think forward to doing better in the Preakness. But all she saw when she closed her eyes was the row of horses that had held them up at the Derby. If that happened in the Preakness, she and Star could be caught again.

Thursday evening Christina lined a row of peas up on her dinner plate, moving the vegetables around so that they formed the same bunching that had held Star up during the Derby. *There's Star,* she thought, rolling a single pea around the plate. Christina replayed the race over and over again in her mind, trying to figure out how she had managed to let Star get boxed in by the other horses. Poor Star, dead last in the biggest race of his life. He deserved better. A better jockey would have put him in a winning position. She had let her precious Star down.

"Christina!" Ashleigh's voice broke into Christina's glum thoughts. "Didn't you hear me?"

Christina looked across the table at her mother and shook her head. "Sorry. What did you say?"

"I said we need to work on our strategy for the Preakness," Ashleigh said, poking a slice of cucumber with her salad fork.

Christina looked back down at her plate and stirred the peas. "I watched the Derby tape again this afternoon, Mom," she said. "I don't know what we could have done any differently." She wished her mother would just let her figure it out for herself. After all, Star was her horse, and she was the one who had blown the race for him.

"I can list a number of things you can do differently," Ashleigh said. "Let's start with when you came out of the gate."

"Let's not," Christina replied, her shoulders tensing as her annoyance with her mother increased. "Star broke from the gate perfectly, Mom."

Ashleigh nodded slowly. "Yes, he did, and it fell apart from there."

Christina gritted her teeth. Didn't Ashleigh know she would do everything she could to make sure things turned out differently in the next race?

"I want to have Star do a few sprints during his works," Ashleigh said. "Let's get that speed going from the start. You can rate him further into the race, once you get away from the pack. We know he has the speed and the stamina to keep ahead if he has the chance."

Christina mashed the peas with the back of her fork, her appetite completely gone. Of course she knew what Star had going for him. She knew Star better than anybody.

"Image seems to be handling her treatment well,"

Mike broke in, leaning back in his chair. "That therapy pool the Townsends have is really something else."

Ashleigh nodded, her expression serious. "I still don't know why Brad is being so generous, but if it weren't for Townsend Acres' medical facility, Image wouldn't stand a chance." She sighed and pushed her plate away. "That filly really ran her heart out for Melanie. They deserved to win the Derby, but what a price to pay."

Christina glanced at her father. She was grateful for his effort to get her mother off the subject of Star's performance in the Derby, but why did he have to pick Image and Townsend Acres as the new topic for conversation? When Ashleigh wasn't after her about the way she had raced Star, she seemed to be finding ways to compare her riding to Melanie's, and that wasn't helping matters in the least.

"I'm done," she announced, picking up her plate. "I'm going upstairs to study."

"Good idea," her father said. "I'll take care of the dishes tonight."

In her room, Christina settled at her desk and opened her world problems textbook. She started to read the dry writing, but her mind kept drifting to Star. Finally she closed the book and rose. *I can read this at the barn*, she told herself. Her parents were in the living room, watching the news, so she slipped quietly out the kitchen door.

When she walked through the barn, the horses were still munching their evening hay. The scents and sounds helped relax her, and Christina gave a contented little sigh as she strode down the aisle. When she reached Star's stall, he popped his head up and pricked his ears at her.

"Move over," she said fondly, opening his stall door. The colt nudged her gently, but when he realized she had no treats for him, he shoved his nose back toward his hay net, pulling out another mouthful. Christina sat cross-legged in a corner of the stall and opened her book again.

After nearly an hour of reading to the sound of Star crunching his hay, she closed the book. "I know as much about world problems as I'm going to," she told the colt, scrambling to her feet. "The bigger problem we have is how to run at Pimlico so that you have a fighting chance."

Star twisted his neck, reaching forward with his back hoof to scratch at his nose. Christina watched him and shook her head. "I guess you don't have any problems," she said. "I'm the one who has to figure things out."

Star angled his head and looked at her, snuffled around his feed pan for any bits of grain he might have missed, then pushed his nose in her direction, demanding a pet.

Christina gently massaged the base of his ears, admiring the soft luster of his red-brown coat. "There was a time when I didn't think you'd ever be able to walk again," she said, stroking his poll. "Things sure have changed since last winter, haven't they?"

Unconcerned, Star made one last attempt to find something more to eat, then turned and nosed Christina's pockets. "And all that matters to you is enough good food in your stomach, right?" Star stomped his hoof, and Christina chuckled. "That, and the chance to run your heart out." And she knew it was up to her to give him that chance.

Christina spent Saturday helping Ian and Ashleigh back several of the two-year-olds. Without Melanie to help, the work of starting the new racehorses fell on Naomi and Christina, while Dani and Joe helped with some of the ground training. Christina wondered how Melanie was handling Image's therapy and life at Townsend Acres. Melanie hadn't been at school since the Derby, but she would be starting again soon, and Christina was sure the Reeses would have heard from her if things were going badly.

Ian held a bay filly's head while Christina lay quietly across her back, letting the young horse get used to the weight of a rider. The filly snorted softly but stood still, trusting the trainer.

Christina's thoughts drifted to her plans for the evening. When she had called Parker to ask him to the prom, he had immediately said yes. Then she had remembered that the formal dance meant getting a dress and shoes. After a frenzied afternoon of last-minute shopping, she and Ashleigh had finally found a dress, but Christina hadn't had much practice walking in the high-heeled dress shoes, and she was still afraid she was going to wobble right off and break her ankle. Which would mean no riding in the Preakness. She stifled a laugh at the thought of being sidelined by a pair of dance shoes. Her movement made the filly jump a little, and Christina quickly turned her attention back to the young racehorse.

"You're fine," she murmured, rubbing her hand on the filly's sleek shoulder.

"That's enough," Ian said, stroking the yearling's arched neck. Christina slid to the ground and stepped back to admire the filly's powerful conformation. "I can hardly wait to get her on the track," she said. "This girl looks like she's going to be a rocket."

"She's doing great," Ashleigh said from the stall door. "We're going to have some fantastic horses running next year."

"I have stalls to clean," Christina said quickly, eager to get away before her mother brought up Star and the Preakness again.

"Don't you have a dance to go to tonight?" Ashleigh asked Christina as she stepped out of the stall.

Christina glanced at her watch and gasped. "I have a million things to do still," she said. "I'd better get going."

She rushed through the rows of stalls she had to clean, throwing forkful after forkful of soiled bedding into the wheelbarrow. By the time she had done her chores, she was damp with sweat and smelled strongly of barn.

She hurried back to the house and jogged up the stairs, trying to remember where she had left the shimmery stockings she'd bought to go with her prom dress. The setting sun shone brightly through the bedroom window, and the pearlescent blue fabric of her formal gown, hanging from the closet door, caught the golden light. Christina gazed at it for a moment. The blue was almost the same color as her racing silks, and her thoughts drifted once again to the nightmare of the Derby. She gave her head a quick shake and began looking through her room for the missing stockings.

"Are these what you're looking for?"

Ashleigh stood in the doorway, holding a flat package.

Christina sighed with relief and hurried over to take the stockings from her mother. "Where were they?" she asked.

"At the barn," Ashleigh said. "Ian found them sitting on my desk."

Christina thought back to the day she'd gone into Lexington to buy the stockings. When she'd gotten home, she had gone straight to the barn to see Star. Now she remembered stopping by Ashleigh's office to glance through the *Daily Racing Form*. An article in the paper had caught her attention. Before checking on Star, she had settled down at the desk to read about a new entry in the Preakness, a chestnut colt called Wild 'n' Free who had an uncanny resemblance to Affirmed, the famous Triple Crown winner. According to the *Daily Racing Form*, the owner, Ghyllian Hollis, had planned to race the colt, bred at Celtic Meadows, in the Derby, but problems with the trainer had kept her from entering her colt. Now Vince Jones, the same trainer who had helped Christina work with Gratis, had taken over Wild 'n' Free's training. In the article, Vince said he was confident that the colt would do well in the Preakness. Christina knew Vince wouldn't be so sure of himself if the horse weren't a great competitor.

"Thank you," she said to Ashleigh, opening the package of stockings. "I'd better hurry up and get dressed."

"You know," Ashleigh said, "I am very proud of what you and Star have accomplished together. Really, Chris, I just want to see both of you do well."

Christina darted a surprised look at her mother. "Thanks, Mom," she said.

Ashleigh left the doorway, and Christina grabbed her towel and headed for the shower. When she pulled on the blue dress, she stood in front of the bathroom mirror and gazed at herself. She wished Melanie and she were getting ready for the dance together. It would have been fun to have Melanie there, helping with her hair and makeup. But Melanie wasn't going to the dance. After several attempts to give some style to her straight hair, Christina gave up, brushing it smooth and pulling it back with a pair of rhinestone hair clips.

Nearly two hours later Christina walked down the stairs, her dress shoes in one hand while she held her floor-length dress up with the other so that she wouldn't trip on the hem. The fabric made soft, whispery sounds as she walked, and she felt as though she should be gliding like a model, not walking as though it were something she had just learned how to do. She paused at the bottom of the stairs to slip her shoes on. *I can gallop a horse at top speed on the track, but I can barely walk in heels,* she thought, grinning to herself as she buckled the dainty straps. She was still laughing at herself when she reached the doorway to the living room.

Parker was sitting on the sofa, deep in conversation with her parents. Christina gazed fondly at him. Parker looked dignified and very handsome in his black tuxedo. He was leaning forward, elbows on his knees, nodding in agreement with whatever Mike was saying. Finally Christina cleared her throat softly, and three heads turned at once.

Parker rose immediately. He stared across the room at her, his eyes wide. A broad grin broke across his face, and Christina smiled back, knowing by his expression that Parker thought she looked great.

"Wow, Chris," Mike said, nodding his approval. "You look wonderful."

"Thanks, Dad," Christina said, starting to feel a little self-conscious under their close scrutiny.

Ashleigh smiled. "That dress is perfect for you, Chris."

A little smile played at the corners of Mike's mouth. "That's an understatement," he said. "There won't be another girl at the dance as beautiful as you." He turned to Parker. "Don't you think so?"

Parker shook his head. "No," he said. "I don't think so."

"What?" Ashleigh and Mike exclaimed at the same time, staring in disbelief at Parker.

Parker turned his attention to Christina again, his eyes sparkling. "I *know* there won't be another girl there as beautiful as you, Chris."

The compliment sent a warm blush up Christina's cheeks. Parker picked a small white box off the coffee table and crossed the room, holding it out to her. She opened the box and took out a corsage of blue carnations and white rosebuds. The flowers were a perfect match for her dress, and she murmured a soft thank-you as she slipped the band onto her wrist.

"We'd better get going," Parker said. "We don't want to miss the start of the dance."

But before they could leave, Mike insisted on taking pictures, so it was several minutes before they stepped onto the porch. Christina's jaw dropped when she saw the blue limousine parked in front of the house. The liveried driver waiting by the passenger door nodded formally to Christina.

"Good evening, miss," he said, opening the door with a flourish. Slowly Christina descended the steps, Parker's arm linked with hers. She wanted to savor every moment of the evening, and so far it was going perfectly.

She settled onto the soft leather bench and smoothed her dress as Parker sat down beside her. When they cruised slowly down the driveway and onto the road, she watched the countryside slip past. The Preakness was less than two weeks away. In spite of her mother's claim that she only wanted the best for Christina and Star, Christina knew that Star's success in the upcoming race would be good for Whitebrook, too. Once again she felt pressure settle onto her shoulders, and she heaved a deep sigh, trying to force herself to forget about racing for the evening.

"A penny for your thoughts."

Parker's voice made her jump, and she turned to him. "I was just thinking of how perfect this evening is going to be," she said. "Thanks for coming with me." She gestured at the interior of the limousine. "This really makes it special."

"It's the least I could do," Parker said. "I'm glad

we're going. I've missed the time we used to spend together."

Christina nodded. "So many things have gotten in the way," she said. "All the stress before the Derby and all of Mel's and my problems have been really distracting for me. With the strain of competing against each other, I feel like I've lost my best friend." She sighed and shook her head. "With what you've been doing with the U.S. Equestrian Team, preparing for the Olympics, and me so wrapped up in racing, there hasn't been time to have any fun at all." She tilted her head and sighed. Then she curled her lips. "And look where it got me." She shook her head. "Before the Derby, I was so stressed out that I was a mental wreck. Then I was so sure of Star and excited about the race. Now I'm dreading the Preakness. What if we blow it again?"

Parker leaned down and dropped a light kiss on her forehead. "You won't," he said in a reassuring tone. "Now let's just enjoy the evening."

When they walked into the high school gymnasium, Christina gasped in surprise. Low lights had been set up to reflect off the silver moon and stars hanging from the ceiling and off the glittery starbursts that decorated the walls, giving the room an intimate, dreamlike quality.

"Wow," she said softly. "This is beautiful."

"It sure is," Parker said, catching her by the elbow and guiding her to a corner where small tables had been set up. Sparkling confetti spilled from stemmed glasses set on mirrored squares on each table, making the cloth-draped cafeteria tables festive.

Christina saw several of her classmates seated at the little tables, laughing and visiting, and she felt out of touch. Even though she'd been invited to a number of recent parties, she'd skipped them. Working with Star and keeping up her grades had been her main concerns. But now she felt out of sync with her friends and classmates. Graduation was less than a month away, and they would all go their separate ways. She wondered how many of them she would ever see again.

Katie Garrity, wearing a gold-colored strapless formal, walked by with her date. Christina realized she didn't know the boy's name. "Katie," she said in greeting, waving at her friend. "You look fantastic."

"Thanks," Katie said. "What do you think of the decorations?" She gestured at the transformed gym.

"Amazing," Parker said. "The dance committee did an excellent job."

"Who came up with the theme?" Christina asked.

Katie's eyes widened and she pinched her mouth shut. "After all the times I told you I'd been put in charge of the prom decorations, you have to ask?" She caught her date's arm. "Um, Allan and I are going to find a table," she said stiffly. "Nice seeing you."

As they walked away, Christina sank low into her chair. "I really blew that one, didn't I?" she said, biting at her lip.

Parker nodded. "I think you hurt Katie's feelings."

"I guess I haven't paid much attention to anything but Star lately," Christina said, plucking a few pieces of iridescent confetti from the champagne glass on their table. "I can't even think beyond two weeks from today and the Preakness."

"Hey, Chris! Parker!" She turned to see Kaitlin Boyce and Gary Smith making their way between the tables. Kaitlin, who took eventing lessons from Parker, was wearing a pink dress with spaghetti straps, her dark hair piled on top of her head.

Christina smiled. "You look wonderful," she told Kaitlin.

"You mean I don't look like I spend most of my time in the stables?" Kaitlin asked with a laugh. She turned to Parker. "Speaking of which, I took good care of Ozzie and Foxy today. And we missed you at class. Samantha took it easy on us this afternoon."

Parker worked for Samantha and Tor Nelson, who owned Whisperwood, where they schooled students and horses in combined training. His job at the farm paid for board on his own eventing horses and helped keep him from being dependent on his parents' money. Teaching there gave him the chance to share his experience with the younger students.

"Thanks, Kaitlin," he said. "I know you take excellent care of those two. And I'll be there for Wednesday lessons, so don't think you're going to have another easy afternoon."

"How's Melanie doing?" Kaitlin asked, turning to Christina. "I was just sick to hear about what happened to Image, but it is so cool that they won the Derby."

"They're both doing pretty well," Christina said, not willing to admit that she hadn't talked to Melanie since the previous Wednesday.

The band started playing, and Kaitlin caught Gary by the arm. "Let's dance," she said, dragging him toward the floor.

"How about you?" Parker asked, turning back to Christina. "Are you ready to dance?"

"I think I'd rather sit this one out," Christina said with a small pout. Now that Kaitlin had brought up Melanie, she couldn't pull her thoughts away from Melanie, Image, and Star.

After the third song, Parker was impatiently tapping his foot to the beat. "Come on," he said. "Let's get on the floor." Christina followed him, trying to recapture the mood she had been in when they left Whitebrook. Once Parker put his arms around her and she started swaying to the music, she felt a little better, but she still didn't really feel part of the scene. Her senior year had gone by in a blur, and she seemed to have missed most of it. She heaved a deep sigh.

"Now what's the problem?" Parker asked, sounding irritated. He led her off the dance floor, and Christina sank back into her chair and watched groups of her classmates talking together, laughing and obviously enjoying themselves. But she couldn't let herself relax.

"I'm stuck on the Derby," Christina admitted.

"You still have two big races ahead of you," Parker said. "You need to think forward, not backward."

Christina rolled her eyes. "I need to understand what went wrong last week," she said.

Parker opened his mouth and took a deep breath, then clamped his lips shut.

"What?" Christina asked sharply.

He shook his head. "I was going to make an observation," he said, "but I changed my mind. I don't think you want to hear it."

"You've never worried about that before," Christina said. "Just spit it out." She leaned across the table to catch Parker by the arm.

Parker closed his eyes and leaned back, then groaned softly. "Your ego got in the way," he said flatly. "I know how it can happen. I've made the same mistake in competition a time or two myself."

Christina bristled at his words. "What do you mean, my ego?" she demanded.

"From what I could see and from the way you talk, I think if you had been more focused on the quality of horses Star was running against and not stuck on the idea that Star deserved to win, you might have done better."

Christina gaped at her friend, shocked by what he had said. "I think you're wrong," she said sharply. She realized that other people could overhear their conversation, and she lowered her voice. "That's not fair, Parker," she said. "I was perfectly aware of the other horses. I helped train Gratis, remember? And I know how good a horse Image is. But I also know that Star is better."

"Then why did they finish in winning positions and Star finish last?" Parker asked quietly.

"I think it's time to go home," Christina said. She rose abruptly and walked out of the gym, not looking back to see if Parker was following her.

Christina sat stiffly on the plush leather seat of the limousine, staring out the window on the way home. Beside her, Parker was silent. When the driver stopped at the Reeses' porch, Christina rested her hand on Parker's arm when he started to get out of the car. "Thank you for the evening, Parker," she said. "You don't have to walk me to the door." The driver opened her door and she started to climb out, then paused. "Thanks for giving me your input on the race." She hurried up the steps, then let herself inside.

The house was dark and silent. Christina was relieved that her parents hadn't waited up for her. She made her way up the stairs quietly. In her room, she peeled off the blue gown and let it fall to the floor in a crumpled heap, then lay across the bed. Too wound up to sleep, she stared at the shadows the moonlight made on the bedroom wall, wondering why life had to be so complicated.

3

CHRISTINA LEANED ON THE TOP RAIL OF THE PRACTICE track, watching Naomi Traeger trotting Charisma, an up-and-coming two-year-old, around the oval. The lean chestnut filly was built like a colt. Ashleigh and Ian had great hopes for Charisma, sired by Wonder's Pride and out of Sun Prism, a mare Mike and Ashleigh had bought at the Keeneland auction. Charisma fought to speed up, dancing her hindquarters sideways, tossing her head eagerly. Naomi kept the filly's nose pointed forward, forcing the excited racehorse to move in a straight line along the rail.

Maureen Mack, the farm's assistant trainer, stood near the opening in the rail, watching closely as the pair circled the oval. She nodded in approval as Naomi brought the filly to a stop nearby. Christina could see the smile on the jockey's face as she hopped off the filly's back and turned to Maureen to discuss their progress.

Christina struggled to recall the feeling she had had when she and Star had started working together—the hope and excitement she had felt about their future on the track. When Star had been so sick the winter before, all she had cared about was saving the colt. Racing had become secondary to keeping Star alive. So why was she feeling so much pressure now about losing the Derby? At least they'd been able to race. That was more than she had been able to hope for when Star had been near death.

"Hey, Christina!"

At the sound of Cindy McLean's voice, Christina turned to see the Tall Oaks trainer and her sister, Samantha Nelson, walking across the yard. Cindy, a retired jockey, had been working with Gratis, Ben al-Rihani's bay colt, since late winter. She and Ben hadn't even had a jockey for Gratis until only a few weeks before the Derby, so Gratis's third-place finish in the race had been a great moment for Tall Oaks.

When Christina had made the decision to pursue her racing career, she had sold her Thoroughbred jumper, Sterling Dream, to Samantha and Tor Nelson.

Knowing that the mare would be loved and well cared for at Whisperwood had made the decision to sell Sterling less distressing for Christina. Kaitlin Boyce had started competing with Sterling, and the pair were doing a great job together.

"Hi, guys," Christina said, smiling at the two women. "How are things at Whisperwood, Sammy?"

Samantha, a fair-skinned redhead, looked a little pale. Christina noticed faint shadows under her eyes, but Samantha smiled broadly. "Great, Chris," she said. "We're busier than ever. Parker's being selected for the USET has brought some good publicity to the farm."

Christina nodded and smiled. She knew that Parker and his horses making it to the Olympic games meant a lot of attention for the Nelsons and their farm.

Samantha rubbed her hand tiredly over her face. "We might have to hire someone just to manage scheduling and run the office," she said. "I can hardly keep up as it is."

"I keep telling her she needs a vacation," Cindy said, frowning at her sister. "You're going to wear yourself out, Sammy."

"I don't have time to be tired," Samantha retorted. "Things will settle down once the Olympics are over and Parker's back to work full time." She eyed Christina. "Speaking of which, how was the dance?"

Christina glanced down at her paddock boots and shrugged. "It was fine," she said in a neutral voice, not eager to talk about her date with Parker. "It's just hard to find time to relax and have fun when there's so much going on."

"I understand that," Cindy said. "When you're working your way up in a competitive sport like racing, you don't have time for anything else."

"You have to wait until you become a trainer and find a nice guy like Ben to work for, right, Cindy?" Samantha asked, poking Cindy's side with her elbow.

Cindy grinned smugly. "That's right," she said, then turned to Christina. "Is your mom in her office?"

Christina nodded. "You mean you didn't come over to spy on the competition?" she asked, nodding toward Naomi and Charisma. Cindy watched the filly closely, and Christina could tell by her expression that she was impressed with the graceful Thoroughbred.

"When Cindy said she was coming over to see your mom about trading some breedings between Tall Oaks and Whitebrook, I thought I'd come along for the ride," Samantha said. "Besides," she added with a grin, "we're thinking about breeding Sterling. Don't

41

you think Jazzman would make the perfect sire for one of Whisperwood's jumpers?"

The big black Whitebrook stallion originally had been trained as a jumper. With his powerful hindquarters and easy temperament, Christina had to agree with Samantha that Jazzman would be an excellent sire for a horse geared for three-day events.

"Awesome," she said, then turned to Cindy. "Aren't you going to use Champion and Khan to cover the Tall Oaks mares?" Cindy and Ben co-owned Wonder's Champion, who had won the Triple Crown when he was owned by Whitebrook and Townsend Acres. Khan had been part of the stock Fredericka Graber sold to Ben when he purchased Tall Oaks the previous winter.

Cindy nodded. "We do plan to use Champion," she said. "But Ben is having his father's stock brought over from Dubai. Most of them have Champion's bloodlines already, so we thought we'd use him on the fillies we're going to pick up this fall at the Keeneland auction, and see if we can work something out with your folks to breed the al-Rihani mares to Whitebrook's other stallions. In a couple of years we'll have Gratis at stud, so with any luck we'll be able to establish ourselves fairly quickly as a serious racing farm, even without a fresh Triple Crown winner."

"Cool," Christina said absently, waving to Naomi as she walked Charisma by, heading for the barns. Naomi smiled and waved in their direction, but her attention was on the energetic filly. "Having Gratis do so well in the Derby was a good start for Tall Oaks."

"I agree," Cindy said. "It's too bad Wolf thinks it was all thanks to his great riding, though." She snorted softly. "He thinks he was pretty impressive. If we put his ego on the scale at the track, he'd be so far over the weight limit that he couldn't afford to pay the over-weight fine."

"But he handled Gratis so well during the race," Christina protested. Ever since Wolf had gone to work for Tall Oaks, it had been obvious that Cindy and Wolf had a personality clash. Christina was sure the only reason they kept working together was because Wolf could manage the colt's unpredictable temperament. Cindy needed to him to race the colt, and as an apprentice jockey, Wolf was getting the opportunity of a lifetime by being allowed to ride in the Triple Crown.

"I know he did a good job handling Gratis in the Derby," Cindy said. "But his placing wasn't all due to his skill. Wolf's a good rider, but he's pretty full of himself, and he pushes things to the limit." She looked closely at Christina. "Speaking of the Derby, how are you doing with Star's training?"

43

"I was just thinking about running away from home," Christina said with a sigh. "There's so much tension around here now, it makes everything that was going on before the Derby seem mild."

Samantha raised her eyebrows in surprise, while Cindy nodded sympathetically. "You and Star are a much better team than your performance showed," she said. "It's a shame things went the way they did."

Christina rolled her eyes. "Mom's been saying the same thing every day for the last week," she said, tilting her head toward the racehorse barn, where Ashleigh spent much of her time. "She's probably in her office right now making diagrams and charts to show me what I need to change for the Preakness."

"She really wants to see you and Star succeed," Samantha said.

"I know," Christina replied. "But she's being such a nag about the whole thing."

"These races mean a lot to Whitebrook," Cindy reminded her. "It isn't just about you and Star."

"How could I possibly forget?" Christina asked. "I hear it every day. Wonder won the Derby, Champion won the Triple Crown, Pride ran his heart out, Star could have been the first colt owned solely by Whitebrook to bring home the crown. But we blew it. And Mom won't let me forget that."

"It sounds like trying to work together with Star is causing problems between you," Cindy commented with a frown.

Christina exhaled heavily. "That's an understatement," she said. "I have finals to prep for, plus all my work here. I'm supposed to graduate in a few weeks, get mentally geared up for the Preakness, and still pretend to be a normal teenager? Ha. I need less pressure right now, but all I'm getting from Mom is more."

"I do understand," Cindy said.

"Me too," Samantha said, pressing her hand to her stomach absently. "I get so caught up with the kids I'm working with, I hate to think of how I'd be if I had one of my own riding in competition. I'd be a wreck."

"Sometimes I think I should never have given up Sterling," Christina said quietly, looking at Samantha. "We might have been part of the USET, heading for the Olympics with Parker, Foxy, and Ozzie."

"You wouldn't give up Star for the world," Cindy said, sounding shocked.

"I know," Christina admitted. "The pressure is just wearing on me. And I already gave up one great racehorse when I sold Legacy to get Sterling." When Ashleigh's Wonder had produced Legacy, Mike and Ashleigh had given Christina their ownership in the Thoroughbred colt. But when Christina made it clear

45

to her mother she was not going to follow in Ashleigh's footsteps and become a jockey, the Reeses' interest in Legacy had been sold so that Christina could get Sterling Dream.

After Star's birth, Christina's change of heart had been her own choice, not one forced upon her by her parents. But at times she questioned that decision. She still thought about jumping, and at times she missed the varied competition of combined training. But at least she knew Sterling was happy, which made it easier to concentrate on racing. At times, though, she wondered what would have happened if she had given Legacy a chance. Maybe the colt would have shown greatness. *Stop thinking like that,* she told herself. *I never connected with Legacy the way I did with Star—it's not the same thing.*

"You know, I saw Legacy's picture in an ad in *Trackside* magazine," Cindy said. "He's standing at stud in New York. He isn't a top draw, but with his bloodlines, he's still a great horse."

"It was a shame that the new owners couldn't work things out with Brad," Samantha said. "Legacy had great potential as a racehorse."

When Ashleigh had been given half ownership of Ashleigh's Wonder, Clay Townsend had also given her half ownership in Wonder's foals. When Brad had taken over Townsend Acres, he had done everything he could to make working together in the horses' best interest impossible. And that included working with the people who had bought the Reeses' interest in Legacy.

Christina rolled her eyes. "As usual, Brad had to make things hard," she said. "They've done so much bickering over training, racing, and jockeys that Legacy never had a chance to prove himself on the track. I know it bothers Mom a lot. We don't even talk about it."

"We'd better get down to the office," Cindy said, offering Christina an encouraging smile. "Don't worry. You'll get through this, Chris, and I'm sure you and Star will have a better race at Pimlico."

"Thanks, Cindy," Christina said.

"We'll be there to cheer you on," Samantha promised.

"That'll be great," Christina said. She watched Cindy and Samantha walk down to the barn, then turned to head for the house. She still had studying to do for finals. Even in the midst of the Triple Crown pressure, she had to get her work done so that she could maintain her grades.

• • •

The following day at school, she slipped into her seat in contemporary world problems just as the bell rang.

Katie Garrity glanced over at her, then looked away without saying a word.

Christina slumped in her chair. She had to find a way to make it up to her friend, but still, she thought Katie could be a little more understanding about how overwhelmed she'd been lately. There was a lot more to life than decorating the gym for the senior prom. But as the teacher began to talk about the current assignment, Christina realized that she was so wrapped up in Star and the races that her senior year seemed to have flown by without her so much as noticing.

She hurried out to the barn as soon as she got home from school. Ashleigh was standing near Star's turnout, gazing thoughtfully at the chestnut colt.

"Is he all right?" Christina asked anxiously when she reached her mother. She still had nightmares about the previous winter, when Star had been too sick even to lift his head and she'd thought she was going to have to have him destroyed. To see her mother watching him so closely brought back all those bad feelings. But when Christina looked at Star, he was grazing contently, looking as fit and healthy as he possibly could.

"He's fine," Ashleigh said. "But we have less than

two weeks before the Preakness. We really need to concentrate on his conditioning and your riding."

"I'm doing everything I can," Christina said tersely. "I still don't know what went wrong in the Derby. All we can do is try again in the Preakness."

"I think you do know what happened," Ashleigh said. "You forgot there were other horses in the race, and you didn't take advantage of the small field to get Star out ahead. There will be more horses running at Pimlico, you know."

Christina bristled. "I know, Mom," she said defensively. "We got caught in the Derby. We couldn't get around the pack. Otherwise Star would have pulled out in front."

Ashleigh shrugged. "I've watched the tape a dozen times," she said. "Maybe you need to sit down and see what you can do differently at Pimlico."

Like I don't already have a million things to do, Christina thought. "I'll watch the race again," she said aloud, then grabbed a grooming bucket and let herself into Star's pasture.

"Don't forget you have some other chores to do," Ashleigh reminded her before she walked away.

Christina groaned to herself. *A million things to do,* she repeated to herself. She couldn't remember the last time she had gone riding just for fun, or really enjoyed getting on a horse's back. It had all become so intense, and she didn't know what she could do to get back to where riding was the greatest thing in world.

Was racing in the Triple Crown really worth the stress and pressure?

CHRISTINA LEANED OVER STAR'S SHOULDERS, BRACED FOR an explosive start from Whitebrook's practice gate. Beside her, Dani was poised over Sassy Jazz's black withers. The mare, an experienced racehorse, snorted and pranced a little, then rolled her eye in Star's direction as though she was checking out her competition.

Star tensed and shifted his hindquarters, preparing for the gate to spring open. Joe stood by the chute, waiting for Ashleigh's signal to release the gate. Christina kept her eyes focused forward, staring over the top rail at the length of track in front of her.

When the gate banged open, Star leaped forward, Sassy at his side. As the horses galloped along the stretch, Christina replayed the Derby. Given a second chance, what would she do? Sassy was between Star and the inside rail. If the horses were equally matched for speed, would she ask Star for a little more at the beginning, to get him ahead and on the inside, or would she hold back and wait for the other jockey to make a mistake so she could get around the other horse?

Push ahead, she told herself. The jockeys riding in the Triple Crown races weren't going to make mistakes to her benefit. The Derby had proven that already. Wolf and Gratis had gotten out front at the start, which had given them the advantage she and Star had missed.

She leaned forward, pressing her hands up Star's neck, keeping the reins taut so that he could balance against the bit. "Come on, boy," she said, urging him to pick up his speed. The colt flicked his ears back and dug in, lengthening his gait, and they pulled ahead of Dani and Sassy.

Christina veered Star closer to the rail and nodded to herself. When they came around the curve of the practice track, Star was several strides ahead of the mare and running easily. *It isn't like Sassy is any competition for Star,* she reminded herself, *but if we come out of the gate running strong, I know Star can keep the lead.* But she saw Ashleigh frowning and shaking her head as they galloped past. *Now what?* she thought, sinking down onto the saddle and cueing Star to slow down. The colt fought her for a moment, still eager to run, and Christina couldn't help but smile. "Save it, boy," she said. "The Preakness isn't too far away. You'll get your chance, I promise."

Finally Star complied. When he dropped to an extended trot, she turned him, and they jogged back to where Ashleigh waited by the outside rail.

"That burst of speed is a good idea," Ashleigh said. "But the Preakness is a mile and three-sixteenths. If you push Star like that at the beginning and try to hold that pace, he might burn out before you're halfway through."

"I'll rate him once we get out front," Christina said, wishing her mother would give her a little credit for knowing how to negotiate the track.

"I don't know," Ashleigh said, shaking her head. "While you get your other chores done I think I'll have Ian sit down with me and review that Derby tape one more time."

Christina groaned to herself. "Watching that stupid tape isn't going to help, Mom," she said, hopping from Star's back.

Dani walked by, leading Sassy back to the barn.

"Do you want me to take Star, too?" she asked Christina.

"No, thanks," Christina replied. "I'll put him up myself."

Joe was moving the practice gate off the track as Naomi led Speedalight, a strongly built two-year-old colt, out to the track, Ian at her side.

"I have to go cool Star out," Christina told her mother. She walked Star away as Ian approached Ashleigh. She didn't want to hear any more about the Derby, her mistakes, or how not to make them again. She could figure it out for herself. Ashleigh's constant pushing was making it hard to focus on riding in the Preakness.

She pulled Star's saddle off and walked him around the yard. The colt nuzzled her shoulder, and Christina glanced at him. "We don't need another lecture on how to ride right, do we, Star?"

Star eyed her, then blew noisily.

"Not you too," she groaned. "I won't let you down, you know. We're going to do everything right in the next race."

After several minutes of easy walking she felt Star's neck. His coat was dry and he was breathing easily, so she put him in the crossties in the barn and gave him a thorough grooming. "You get to enjoy the day just relaxing," she told him, leading him to his paddock. "I still have loads of work to get done before I go to school."

After putting Star out, she walked over to the barn where the young racehorses were waiting. She grabbed a lunge line from the tack room, then clipped a lead onto Royal Blue's halter and led the colt out to the round pen. After warming him up with several circuits at a walk, she urged the young horse into a smooth jog.

"That's a good boy," Christina said, tapping at the colt's hip with the tip of her lunge whip. Royal tossed his head, tugging at the hold she had on the line, but he circled Christina at a steady pace, keeping the line tight as he moved around her. She admired the colt's action. His long strides and smooth gait made her think of Star at that age. "You're going to be one fast horse," she told the colt. He snorted, then gave a playful buck and jerked his head, giving the line a powerful yank.

"Enough of that!" she exclaimed, tugging the line firmly. She gestured with the whip again, urging Royal to pick up his speed. "If you have the energy to play around like that, you can put it into working a little harder," she scolded the colt.

Royal snorted loudly and rolled his eyes, but he lengthened his stride and continued to trot. When

Christina changed hands and asked him to turn so that he could work on the opposite lead, the colt obeyed without hesitation. "You sure look good," she told him, admiring his even strides. "Maybe in two years you'll be running in the Kentucky Derby."

"Does this mean you're giving up on Wonder's Star?"

At the strange voice, Christina jumped. Her sudden move startled Royal, who snapped his head up and broke into a gallop, jerking hard on the lunge line. "No!" Christina cried. She struggled hard to stop the colt. She had visions of leg injuries and bowed tendons as the colt tossed his head and pounded his feet on the ground. Finally she regained control of the session and brought him to a stop, then had him walk to her. She rubbed his nose and ran her hand down his sweaty shoulder, bending down to feel his legs. When she finally straightened, she whipped around to face the intruder, immediately recognizing the man as a reporter from the local paper.

"What can you tell me about Perfect Image's recovery?" the man asked, leaning over the fence and holding out a microphone. "How's Melanie Graham dealing with her own injuries? Will she be racing for another stable in the Preakness? Have you decided to pull Wonder's Star from the race? After the Derby, people are wondering if you want to risk any more humiliation."

Christina felt her jaw drop. She stared at the reporter, unable to form a coherent sentence. As she gaped stupidly at him, she felt her anger grow. "You need to leave," she said sharply, then clamped her mouth shut. Whatever she said would be put into quotes and printed. She had learned that keeping her comments short and to the point was the only way to respond to the kinds of questions this man was asking.

"What about Image?" the reporter demanded.

"I'm working right now," Christina said, moving between the reporter and Royal. "I have to take care of my horse, and I don't have time for an interview. I'm sure you know the way off the property." With that she turned away to lead the colt from the pen. She forced herself not to hurry back to the barn. She didn't look back to see if the reporter had left or not. Her hands were trembling as she walked Royal, checking him frequently to see if he was cooled down enough to groom. When she was done brushing him, she carefully wrapped his legs, still concerned about his short gallop in the pen.

The day at school went by in a blur. As Christina was leaving her advanced-placement English class, the teacher, Mrs. Smith, gestured for her to stop.

Christina walked up to the desk and waited for Mrs. Smith to finish talking to Erin Weatherly, another senior.

"I understand you've decided against college," Mrs. Smith said to Christina when Erin walked away.

Christina nodded. "Maybe next year," she said. "Right now I just want to concentrate on the work I'm doing."

"It would be a shame for you not to go on to higher education," the teacher said, holding out a handful of papers. "Your work in my class has been so impressive. I would love to see you go on to college and get a degree in English. Maybe you could be a journalist and write for one of the track papers. That way you could still be involved in what you love to do."

Christina blinked, stunned by Mrs. Smith's suggestion, especially after that morning's confrontation. She hated reporters. They were so pushy and rude, and then only wrote what they wanted to.

Christina smiled politely. "Thanks for the encouragement," she said, then hurried from the classroom. Just what she needed—more pressure. Outside the door she leaned against the wall, waiting for the crush of students swarming between classes to clear before she headed for her next class. She saw Melanie walking by, talking with Katie Garrity. Melanie glanced in her direction, flashed her a brief, distracted smile, and continued on. Christina sank back against the wall, trying not to feel hurt that her cousin didn't even stop to say hi. After all, Melanie was as busy as she was, working on helping Image heal. And Christina knew deep down that she had avoided going over to Townsend Acres to see Melanie because their friendship had been pretty strained before Image broke down. Christina wasn't sure if Melanie would want to see her or not.

The following morning when she came downstairs, both her parents were still down at the barn. The house seemed eerily quiet without Melanie around. Christina thought briefly about calling her cousin, but when she headed for the kitchen phone, she saw the newspaper on the table, folded open to an article with a bold headline that read "Wondering About Wonder's Star." Christina instantly forgot about calling Melanie. Instead she sank onto a chair and began reading the article.

Christina Reese, the young owner and jockey of Wonder's Star, doesn't seem to have much of a future in racing. Reese's last-place showing in the Kentucky Derby seems to indicate the direction of her short career as a jockey. After so much attention to the Whitebrook colt's miraculous come-

back last winter, Reese and Star seem to have faded into the background. Without the experience and maturity needed to succeed, Ms. Reese will burn out fast. Star, the last foal out of the Derby winner Ashleigh's Wonder, seems to be ending his own racing career with a fizzle.

Another former Whitebrook jockey, Melanie Graham, is pulling out of her own devastating setback with a good attitude and determination. Ms. Graham is working with Perfect Image, the amazing filly who won the Kentucky Derby only to break down as she crossed the finish line. Ms. Graham is staying at Townsend Acres, where Image is being treated at the farm's medical facility. Both the filly and jockey are recovering from their traumatic injuries in the Derby. "I won't let a few broken ribs slow me down," Ms. Graham told this reporter. "And Image will pass her winning spirit on to her foals. Her owner, Jazz Taylor, and I are looking forward to continued success on the track."

After reading Melanie's quote, Christina shoved the paper aside. Melanie might not be as skilled as Christina, but she had focus and determination.

She stormed down to the barn, the paper in her hand. When she reached Ashleigh's office, she thrust the article in front of her mother. Ashleigh read the text, then grimaced. "Not exactly a great article, was it?" she asked.

"That's an understatement," Christina said, flopping into a chair near the door. "That reporter really flamed me and Star."

"You can't pay any attention to one writer's opinion," Ashleigh said. "Don't let the media distract you, Chris. You need to concentrate on Star and your riding."

"I'm trying!" Christina exclaimed. "But how can I get away from the fact that Star and I did such a lousy job in the Derby and everyone is putting pressure on me to do better?"

Ashleigh sighed heavily. "Maybe you need to put some pressure on yourself instead of hiding behind the loss," she said. "Limit your focus to riding your very best and keeping the Preakness competition in mind."

Christina felt as though she were going to burst. She jumped from her chair. "I have finals to deal with," she said brusquely. "I'm supposed to be ready for the tests and at the same time deal with graduation and my future—which," she said, holding up the paper, "the press doesn't think includes racing."

"Calm down," Ashleigh told her in a firm tone. "You're letting everything get to you."

"Of course I am," Christina said. "How can I not?"

"By limiting your focus," Ashleigh said. "You need

to work with Star and get through the Preakness. Your grades are good. They always have been. You'll do fine on your finals."

Christina started to open her mouth, then thought better of it. "You don't understand," she mumbled as she left the office. "No one does."

5

"I'M SO GLAD YOU DECIDED TO COME OVER," MELANIE SAID in greeting when she opened the door of the guest cottage.

Christina held out a paper sack. "Dad baked some cookies for you," she said. "And there's a nice apple for Image, too."

"Thanks," Melanie said, taking the sack. "Living here at Townsend Acres is pretty luxurious, but I'm getting tired of my own cooking." She gestured for Christina to step inside.

"Good idea," Christina said, darting a furtive glance over her shoulder before she walked inside. *Cottage* was hardly the best description for this house, a two-story stone-and-cedar building with a wide flagstone porch and white-painted railings. "I don't think Bradley Whiplash is skulking around," she said in a mock whisper. "But you never know when he's going to show up, twirling his mustache."

Melanie stared at her, not so much as smiling at the joke.

"Brad's been very good to me," she said, shutting the door behind them. "It's hard to get used to, because it seems so out of character. I was accustomed to him being rude and arrogant. But everyone here has gone out of their way to make me feel at home."

Christina was surprised to hear Melanie defending Brad Townsend. "Aren't you the least bit suspicious about his motives?" she asked.

Melanie shook her head, leading the way to the kitchen. "Maybe Brad's starting to realize that it doesn't hurt to be nice," she said, setting the sack of cookies on the counter.

Christina doubted it, but she kept the thought to herself. "You look great," she told her cousin, eager to change the subject. "How's your rib doing?"

Melanie lightly touched her side and shrugged. "Still a little tender," she said. "But the doctor said it's healing fast." She sighed. "I'm recovering a lot faster than Image, but she's doing amazingly well, too."

"Can I see her?" Christina asked. She had seen the

filly being worked in the Townsends' therapy pool when Image had come out of her anesthesia after surgery, but that had been a while ago.

"Of course," Melanie said. "You won't believe the progress she's made. Let's walk over to the barn." Melanie plucked the apple from the sack, and they left the cottage by the kitchen door.

Melanie led the way along a gracefully curved stone path that led to the barn attached to the pool. Christina looked around at the beautifully landscaped grounds, then thought back to the gravel paths and simple fences that surrounded Whitebrook. "It's going to be hard for you to come back to Whitebrook after living here," she told her cousin.

Melanie hesitated, then nodded slowly. "It is really nice here," she said. "I could get used to this without even trying."

"Whitebrook seems really quiet without you," Christina said.

Melanie glanced over her shoulder and raised her eyebrows. "Wasn't that part of the problem when I was there?" she asked. "Too much going on with Image at the farm?"

Christina exhaled heavily. "It was pretty stressful for everyone," she said. "But that was before the Derby. Things have calmed down a lot."

"Before Image was a has-been, you mean," Melanie said.

Feeling an argument coming on, Christina let the comment drop. She saw Parker's truck near the barn, hitched to his horse trailer, and let her gaze linger in that direction.

"Parker's been a great friend," Melanie commented.

"Do you see him very often?" Christina asked, trying to sound as though she didn't really care. Parker's comment that she had thought Star deserved to win still irritated her, but her mother had said the same thing. And she was beginning to wonder whether it had upset her so much because they spoke the truth.

"Parker isn't around all that much," Melanie said. "He's at Whisperwood most of the time, working with Foxy and Ozzie when he's not teaching. He keeps as busy as we do. Or as I used to," she amended, touching her hand to her side. "I can hardly wait to get cleared to ride again."

Melanie pushed open the door to the stable attached to the rehabilitation barn, and Christina followed her inside. Large fans stirred the air, keeping the building an even temperature. The stall walls were solid, so that the horses were not exposed to each other

66

or to visitors in the aisle. Christina knew it made sense for health reasons, for security reasons, and to keep the barn pristine, but she didn't like being shut off from the animals.

They strode along a wide concrete aisle until Melanie stopped in front of a stall door. "Hey, sweetie," she cooed as she opened the latch and swung the heavy wooden door open. "How's my girl?"

Christina peeked around Melanie to see Image standing calmly in the stall. "She looks so relaxed," Christina commented, amazed at how good the filly looked.

Image flicked her ears in their direction.

"She's getting plenty of exercise," Melanie explained. "That pool is the greatest thing in the world." She stepped inside the stall and rubbed Image's shiny black nose. "Besides," she added, "the vet has her on a low dose of tranquilizer to keep her mellow."

Christina thought back to when Raven had been injured. It had been a nightmare keeping the White-brook filly calm in her stall for weeks until her leg healed. "I wish we could have a rehab barn at White-brook, too," she said. "It would be cool to be able to help the injured animals recover."

"It has been really interesting, hanging around here," Melanie said. "I've learned a lot from helping the vet and working with a couple of the other horses who are using the therapy pool."

Image nickered softly, and Melanie glanced at her watch. "It's almost time for her session in the pool," she said. "Do you want to stick around and see me work with her?"

"I can't," Christina said. "I still have work to do at home. I just wanted to see how you two were doing here."

"And see if Parker was around?" Melanie asked in a teasing voice.

"No," Christina replied. She didn't know if there was a chance that she and Parker could ever get back together, considering their insane schedules and their different focuses with horses. It was better just to leave that part of her life alone. "I'd better get going."

"I'm going to stay here and get Image ready for her treatment," Melanie said. She gave Christina a quick hug. "It was great to see you, Chris."

"You too," Christina said, then left the barn, hoping that on her way out she wouldn't meet up with Brad or, even worse, Lavinia Townsend.

She made it to her car without seeing anyone, and she breathed a sigh of relief as she headed down the brick-lined driveway. *Back to the reality of Whitebrook,* she told herself, pulling onto the road.

· · ·

The next morning she was up at dawn, even though it was Saturday. She hurried out to the barn, crunching an apple as she walked down the gravel path. She fed Star the rest of the apple while she groomed him, and in a few minutes she had him tacked up for his work-out.

After several minutes of warming the colt up, she jogged him around the track until he was sweating lightly. Ashleigh was waiting by the rail, a stopwatch in her hand, and at her signal, Christina pushed Star into a gallop, counting the poles as they flew along the track's inside rail. When she pulled him up after four furlongs, the colt was still breathing easily. She walked him out to cool him down a little before riding him to where her mother was waiting.

"He looks great," Ashleigh said, smiling up at Christina, who sat lightly on the colt's back. Christina patted Star's neck, feeling the heat coming off him after their early morning work. Ashleigh held up her stopwatch for Christina to see.

When she saw the fractions Ashleigh had clocked, Christina grinned broadly. "He's in perfect shape," she said, feeling better about the colt than she had in sev-eral days.

Ashleigh's smile faded. "He is," she agreed. "But we still need to work on your technique for the Preakness. The other jockeys have so much more experience, it's going to be extra hard for you to compete."

Christina tightened her lips, feeling as though her mother had just set weights on her back. "Mom," she exclaimed, "lighten up! Star and I will be fine. I want to win, too, you know."

Ashleigh reached up to knead the back of her neck, her gaze steady on Christina's face. "I know you and Star have been through a lot to get to this point," she said. "I'm just afraid you're not seeing the Triple Crown races as the fierce competition that they are. I do hope you treat the next two races with a little more respect."

Christina inhaled sharply, but before she could say anything else, her mother walked away.

Christina hopped from Star's back, forcing herself to take deep, steady breaths to calm her anger. She couldn't believe her mother thought she had taken a win in the Derby for granted. That wasn't what had happened on the track. She led Star to the barn and put his halter on, then put him in the crossties so she could untack and groom him properly.

The colt huffed softly, blowing warm air into her face, and she paused to kiss his soft nose.

"If I were a horse, would I get that kind of attention from you?"

Startled by the sound of Parker's voice, Christina turned. "What are you doing here?" she asked, surprised to see him.

Parker smiled sheepishly. "After our date ended on such a sour note, I thought I'd try to make peace with you," he said, holding out a bouquet of yellow carnations. "Do these help?"

Christina couldn't stop the smile that spread across her face. "Thank you," she said. "Even without the flowers, I'm glad you stopped by."

"I was on my way over to Whisperwood," Parker said. "I thought you might like to go see Foxy and Ozzie with me." Foxglove, Parker's mare, and Wizard of Oz, nicknamed Ozzie, were the two horses Parker was using to compete in the Olympics as a member of the USET.

"I'd love to," Christina said. "But I have to groom Star first."

"I'll give you a hand," Parker said. "I'll grab a grooming bucket."

They both went to work brushing Star.

"I'm worried about the way my dad is manipulating Melanie," Parker said as he worked a rubber currycomb along Star's flank. "It's so obvious to me that he's up to something, but she can't see it."

"I know," Christina said. "Right now Mel is so worried about Image that she doesn't want to think your dad has some devious plan up his sleeve, and there's nothing I can say to convince her otherwise. Besides," she said, "if your dad hadn't let Mel use the pool and the equipment at Townsend Acres, she would have lost Image."

Parker looked grim. "I guess we'll have to keep an eye on things and hope something new sidetracks the old man before he convinces Jazz that Townsend Acres should own at least a half interest in Image."

Christina nodded. "Some of his schemes do backfire, remember."

Parker peered over Star's back and grinned at Christina. "Like him selling his interest in Star to you because he thought Star was a goner?"

Christina grinned back. "Exactly."

With both of them working on the colt, Star's grooming went quickly.

"Do you still want to come over to Whisperwood with me?" Parker asked as they walked Star to his turnout. "Maybe a change of scenery would do you good."

Christina slipped Star's halter off his nose and

gave the colt's forelock a light tug. "From horses to . . . horses?" She laughed. "That does sound like fun. I haven't seen Sterling for a long time."

Christina got Star settled in his stall, then quickly cleaned up and hopped into Parker's truck. When they reached Whisperwood, Parker stopped his pickup near the barn and Christina climbed out, pausing to gaze around the combined training facility. "Things have changed since last time I was here," she said, looking at a new arena, set up with several gaudy jumps.

"That was after Captain Donnelly gave Sam and Tor some suggestions to upgrade their training program," Parker said. "Having connections with the chef d'equipe for the USET has been really good for the farm." Captain Donnelly had used the grounds at Whisperwood to work with some of his team members before the Rolex competition, which had brought more good publicity to the Nelsons' farm.

"Tor and I built some of the types of jumps they used at Rolex so we can get the kids and their horses used to going over things that are a little out of the ordinary," Parker explained, pointing out a large ring-shaped jump that was festooned with flapping ribbons.

Christina nodded, remembering some of the odd

things that she had ridden Sterling over during the time they had been competing. "That's such a great idea," she said.

"Parker, Christina!" Kaitlin Boyce came out of the barn, leading Sterling. The mare was saddled and ready to ride, and Kaitlin had her helmet in her hand.

Christina smiled at the younger girl. Kaitlin was one of Parker's best students, eager to do well. She and Sterling made a good team, although Christina felt a slight tug of envy. She loved racing, but she did miss spending time on Sterling, facing the challenge of the eventing courses they had ridden together. "It looks like we're in time to see you and Sterling work," she said.

Kaitlin buckled her helmet into place and nodded. "She is *such* an awesome horse," she said, giving the mare's gray neck an affectionate pat before lowering her stirrups. Christina rubbed Sterling's soft nose while Kaitlin hopped onto the saddle. Christina stepped aside and watched Kaitlin ride toward the warm-up ring.

"Where are Foxy and Ozzie?" Christina asked Parker as Kaitlin circled the ring, letting Sterling stretch her legs at a walk.

"In their turnouts," Parker said. "Let's go see them while Kaitlin gets Sterling warmed up."

They walked around the barn, where Tor was on his back with his head under one of the farm's horse trailers. "Hi, guys," he said, waving a wrench in the air. "Never mind me. When I'm not head steeplechase coach, vet's assistant, and hoof picker, I'm the resident mechanic."

"Is there something you need help with?" Parker asked.

Tor shook his head. "Just making sure the trailer is in tip-top condition," he said.

"Where's Sam?" Christina asked, looking around for Tor's wife.

"In the house," Tor said. "She's been feeling a little under the weather lately, so she's taking a nap."

"I hope it isn't anything serious," Christina said quickly, thinking of how pale Samantha had looked the day she and Cindy came to Whitebrook.

Tor shook his head. "No," he said. "She's doing just fine."

"We'll let you get back to work, then," Parker said.

Tor touched the end of the wrench to his forehead in a mock salute. "Thank you for your permission, Mr. Townsend," he said, grinning.

Parker led Christina around the barn to the paddock where Ozzie, Parker's bay hunter, was grazing peacefully. When he heard them, the gelding popped his head up and pricked his ears in their direction, then crossed the field to greet them.

"You're sure Mr. Friendly," Christina commented, playfully tugging at Ozzie's lower lip. Parker pulled a mint from his pocket and handed it to the horse, who worked it around his mouth for a minute before crunching into it.

"He's amazing," Parker said, smiling proudly. "I still can't believe I own him."

"I know," Christina said. "Like me owning Star. It still doesn't seem real." She patted Ozzie's fuzzy neck. "It's strange to think that just a couple of years ago I was going to be competing with you at three-day events, making my mark with Sterling. Now look at us."

"That's right," Parker said. "Just look at us, a top jockey and an Olympic competitor."

They walked over to the adjoining pasture, where Parker's mare, Foxglove, was waiting at the rail. She sniffed Parker's hands impatiently and stomped her foot. "You saw me give Ozzie that mint," Parker said, digging another piece of candy from his pocket. Foxy caught it with her lips and ate it noisily, then lowered her head to eye Parker as if asking for another treat.

"Forget it," he said, running his hand down her

nose. "Let's go back and see if Kaitlin has Sterling in the jumping ring yet."

By the time they returned to the arena, Samantha was at the rail, watching Kaitlin take Sterling around the ring.

"Hey, stranger," Samantha said, smiling warmly at Christina. "Just because you're not jumping anymore doesn't mean you can't come by to visit."

Christina smiled weakly. "I know," she said. "I'm just so busy, it doesn't seem I have time for anything."

Samantha nodded in understanding. "I know someone else in the same situation," she said, giving Parker a quick look before turning her attention back to Christina. "How are things going with you and your mom?"

Christina grimaced. "I'm getting lectured about my riding every time she sees me," she said with a resigned sigh.

"So it isn't any better?"

"Nope." Christina didn't want to discuss her mother's attitude about the Triple Crown races at the moment. She watched Kaitlin urge Sterling into a smooth canter and approach the first jump. Christina felt another tug of wistfulness as Kaitlin balanced in her stirrups, positioning herself over the mare's withers as they approached a three-foot oxer. Sterling sailed lightly over the low jump and cantered on. Christina could feel herself in the saddle, that incredible sense of weightlessness that came with the impulsion of the horse taking flight. She sighed softly.

"Do you miss it?" Parker asked, his attention on Kaitlin and Sterling.

"Sometimes," Christina admitted. "Especially after races like the Derby."

Parker grinned down at her, his eyes bright. "That's how I feel after a lousy day's competition, too," he said. "I start thinking I should have done something else, something where I wouldn't have to know what it feels like to lose."

Christina chuckled at the words. "That's exactly what I was thinking," she said, shaking her head. "I guess losing is a part of competing, no matter what you do."

Parker shrugged. "Don't tell my dad that," he said in a mock whisper. "He's the biggest whiner in the world when things don't go his way."

"I've noticed," Christina said, then glanced at her watch. "I'd better get home," she said. "I have chores to do this afternoon. Thanks for bringing me over here, Parker."

When Parker gave her hand a light squeeze, Christina wanted to cup his cheek in her hand and give him a quick kiss, but she stopped herself. *Parker and I are just friends now, not a steady couple, right?* She smiled up at him instead, then turned and led the way back to the pickup.

6

CHRISTINA PARKED THE BLAZER IN FRONT OF CINDY'S cottage. When she got out of the rig she paused to gaze around the grounds of Tall Oaks before walking up the flagstone path that led to the trainer's house. Farther up the winding driveway, on a large knoll overlooking the property, sat the main house, a massive brick colonial.

Cindy's home, the old caretaker's cottage, was a smaller version of the mansion, with the same columns and brickwork decorating the entry. While not quite as grand as Townsend Acres, Tall Oaks was still much more elegant than Whitebrook. Both the main house and the cottage had new roofs and fresh paint on the woodwork, with perfectly manicured landscaping around them. Ben took great pride in keeping everything on the old estate authentic and in excellent repair. Even the barns, while thoroughly modernized, had been enhanced with brickwork and rooflines that matched the houses.

While she was admiring the way Ben and Cindy had fixed up the farm, Christina saw Cindy walking from the farm's practice track toward the main barn. She turned away from the cottage and started in that direction.

"Hey, Christina! Hold on!"

She stopped when she heard Wolf call her name, and looked over her shoulder to see Gratis's jockey jogging down the concrete drive, wearing baggy gym shorts and a tank top. He stopped when he reached her, breathing heavily. Sweat streamed down his face and chest, soaking the front of his shirt.

"Good workout," Wolf said with a grin, swiping at the rivulets of perspiration that streaked his face.

"You look like you just sweated off about five pounds," Christina observed.

"I'm keeping in shape for the Preakness," Wolf said, flexing his arm to show off his biceps.

Christina thought about her own nonexistent exercise program. She needed to start working out regularly again. *In my spare time,* she added mentally. "I was just heading for Cindy's office," she told Wolf.

Wolf fell in step beside her as she started toward the barns again. "Cindy's been a little irritable lately," he said. "You'd think my bringing Gratis in third at the Derby would have made her happy." He shook his head in disgust. "Considering that if it hadn't been for me, the horse wouldn't even have been on the track, you'd think she would be grateful. Instead she thinks she needs to criticize every little thing I do with the horse now."

Unable to help herself, Christina started to laugh. Wolf glared at her. "I'm not laughing about Cindy nagging you," Christina said quickly. "But that is exactly what I was telling Cindy about my mom. I can't so much as saddle Star without her standing right there telling me what I'm doing wrong. You'd think I'd never ridden before!"

Wolf raised his eyebrows. "Maybe it's just trainers," he said.

"I don't think so," Christina replied. "Not in my case, anyway."

"I'll see you later," Wolf said when they neared the barn. He headed for the tack room, where there was a shower and small dressing room, and Christina walked into the barn, where Cindy kept her office.

She saw Cindy at the far end of the building, talking to Elizabeth and Beckie, two of the employees at Tall Oaks. When she got close, Beckie offered her a friendly grin. "Hi there, stranger," she said, waving enthusiastically.

Cindy turned and gave her a warm smile, then looked back at Elizabeth and Beckie. "Taking care of the rest of the tack and getting the storage room reorganized should take up the rest of the afternoon," she told the girls.

"We're on our way," Elizabeth said. "See you later, Chris," she said. "The slave driver isn't giving us a moment's peace."

Cindy made a gagging sound. "It took me years to get into a position where I could boss other people around," she teased the two girls. "And I'm not going to waste a moment of it!"

As Elizabeth and Beckie walked away Cindy gestured for Christina to follow her to her office. "I saw that awful article about you and Star," she said as she sat down at her desk.

Christina shuddered. "I couldn't believe what that guy wrote," she said, folding her arms across her chest as she leaned against the door jamb. "He couldn't wait to rip into us."

"The reporter is an idiot," Cindy said flatly. "I know it's hard to read that stuff, but I wouldn't put a lot of stock in his article. He was just looking for a new angle to cover. But still," she added, "it's annoying, to say the least."

Christina nodded. Unlike Ashleigh, Cindy really did seem to understand. "Mom says to just ignore the papers," she said. "But when they're saying good things, she can't stop talking about how great the media is for giving us good coverage."

Cindy nodded. "It's easy to tell someone not to let the media get to them," she said. "I know how that goes. When I had to quit racing, every reporter who knew anything about the track had some nasty comment to make about my shoulder injury. And you know what?" she said, leaning forward. "Not one of them so much as interviewed me before they wrote the things they did." She shook her head. "It is really hard." She sank back and smiled sympathetically. "But it could be worse."

"How?" Christina asked.

"You could have done well in the race and still had them ripping into you."

"What do you mean?"

Cindy pointed at a paper sitting on the edge of her desk. "The writers are saying my jockey placed the way he did by sheer luck." She sighed. "The terrible thing about it is, a lot of what they're saying is true."

Christina thought about Wolf complaining about Cindy, and she kept her mouth shut.

"Wolf is a good rider," Cindy said. "Don't get me wrong there. If I hadn't truly believed he could handle the race, we would have pulled Gratis from the Derby."

"What's wrong with his riding?" Christina asked.

"I don't think he's got enough experience to ride a good clean race," Cindy said. "He uses some unorthodox techniques to keep his horse out front."

"Does that mean you're going to pull Gratis from the Preakness?" Christina asked. "That would be so unfair to the horse."

"I don't plan to withdraw him," Cindy said. "I really was pleased with Gratis's standing in the Derby. I didn't even hope for him to do as well as he did. But I think it would be helpful for Wolf to spend more time working around some other jockeys and exercise riders so his ego doesn't get him and Gratis into trouble. I'm trying to squeeze in a few races for him before next week, but I don't have any other horses to race right now, and his mouth gets him in trouble with the other trainers. They don't like his attitude any more than I do."

"Maybe you should send him over to Whitebrook," Christina said with a wry chuckle. "I'm sure Mom could take him down a few notches."

Cindy grinned. "You and Ashleigh are still bickering, huh?"

"That's an understatement!" Christina said. "If I get one more critical comment from her, I swear my brain is going to explode."

At that, Cindy started to laugh. "What an image," she said. "Just wear your helmet, okay?"

Christina thought about it and started to laugh, too, then shook her head. "It's really tough having Mom as my trainer," she said. "I know she means well, but she only makes it worse for me sometimes, not better."

Cindy nodded in understanding. "She's too close to you," she said. "I can see where you two might have some conflicts at this point." She raised her eyebrows. "Maybe I *should* send Gratis and Wolf to your mom and you and Star can train here."

"So, how's Gratis doing?" Christina asked. She had ridden Gratis several times the previous winter and had developed a good rapport with the big bay colt. His third-place finish in the Derby had not surprised Christina. Gratis was powerful and fast. With the right jockey on board, the bay colt could do great things. The trouble was finding someone who could work with him. Wolf was one of the few people who had managed to control the willful horse. With a more experienced jockey than Wolf, Gratis could have won the race. *Of course,* Christina reminded herself, *I could say the same thing about Star.*

"Right this way," Cindy said, rising and leading the way out of the office and down the barn aisle. "Sometimes I wonder if having both Alydar and Affirmed in his bloodlines gives Gratis the quirky personality traits he likes to flaunt."

"What do you mean?" Christina asked. She knew the colt had excellent breeding, but he was also irascible and difficult to handle. It had taken her a long time to earn the colt's trust and be able to ride him with any success.

"Affirmed and Alydar had one of the most famous rivalries on the track," Cindy said, sliding the barn door open. They stepped into the mid-May sunlight. "Right down to the Derby, when Alydar was the favorite going in. Gratis has that same attitude Affirmed had, where he only does as much as he needs to, but he also has Alydar's courage and hates to be beaten."

"Maybe he needs a horse psychologist to help him be less conflicted," Christina suggested with a laugh.

Cindy laughed, too. "If we could only get those two sides to his personality to work together, he'd run the legs off any other horse on the track."

As they approached the smooth white fence surrounding Gratis's paddock, Cindy called, "Hey, big guy." The colt took another bite of grass, then slowly raised his head to glance in their direction.

"See what I mean?" Cindy said. "He's got the biggest attitude in the world."

"He *is* arrogant," Christina commented with a chuckle.

Cindy curled her upper lip and cast a sour look at Christina. "Maybe that's why he and Wolf do so well together," she said. "They've both got enough arrogance for a whole field of horses and riders."

"But Wolf did such a great job for you," Christina protested.

Cindy nodded. "He keeps telling me that," she said. "I can only hope he does as well in the Preakness. The exposure would be great for the farm. It's going to take a while for us to recover the reputation Tall Oaks had at one time."

While Fredericka Graber had owned Tall Oaks, her farm manager, Alexis Huffman, had nearly driven the farm into bankruptcy, and caused Mrs. Graber to sell most of its good stock. Ben and Cindy were determined to make Tall Oaks one of the most renowned Thoroughbred farms in the country, no matter how many years it took to reestablish the farm's reputation.

Gratis began moving toward the fence, pausing to take a nip of grass every few steps. When he reached Cindy and Christina, he lifted his head and took a bite at Christina's arm.

"Hey!" she exclaimed, quickly flicking his nose with her fingertip. "Knock it off, you monster."

Gratis tossed his head, curling his lip back as though he were laughing, which made both Cindy and Christina chuckle. "You're a big brat," Christina said to the racehorse, who gave a loud snort and wheeled away to prance several steps into the field before he stopped and began grazing again.

"I'd better get home," Christina said. "I have tons of work to do, and I'm sure Mom will be after me to review some old race tapes or some such helpful exercise."

Cindy patted her shoulder. "Good luck," she said. "I have some phone calls to make. Ben and I are going to visit some of the farms that are bringing yearlings to the Keeneland sale next fall. I want to check out all the stock I can before the auction."

"Have fun," Christina said. "I'll see you later." Visiting some of the large farms would be a great way to spend an afternoon or two. Cindy and Ben were so lucky to have found each other. She thought about Parker, heading for the Olympics, and wondered if they had any hope of ever making a relationship work. Even though she was so busy she could barely think, she still missed Parker and the things they used to do together.

When she reached Whitebrook, she went straight to the house and called Townsend Acres.

"Mr. Parker isn't home," the maid who answered the phone informed her. "Can I take a message?"

"That's okay," Christina said. "Thanks anyway." She hung up and strolled down to the barn, where she found both her parents standing outside Star's turnout.

"What's going on?" she asked when she reached the fence.

"We were just discussing an odd phone call I got this afternoon," Ashleigh said, giving Christina a quizzical look.

"About Star?" Christina asked, looking at the colt anxiously. Star looked peaceful and content, his eyes half closed, one hind leg cocked as he dozed in the afternoon sun.

"Sort of," Mike replied. "About you and Star, actually."

Puzzled, Christina looked from one parent to the other, waiting for an explanation.

"Cindy called me," Ashleigh said. "She suggested

that you move Star to Tall Oaks so that you and Wolf can work Star and Gratis together for a few days." She frowned at Christina. "Where would she have gotten an idea like that?"

Christina swallowed, startled by the question. "I— I'm not sure," she stammered. She hadn't expected Cindy to take her seriously when she complained about Ashleigh.

"What she said makes sense," Mike interjected. "She thinks both colts would keep a better edge if they're getting a sense of competition from each other, and it would do both you and Wolf good to work around each other on the track."

Ashleigh nodded, not looking convinced. "I have my doubts," she said. "We know what Star can do. He proved himself in the Louisiana Derby, as far as I'm concerned. On the other hand," she continued, "Gratis and Wolf did place in the Derby, and Star wasn't exactly shining that day."

Christina pressed her mouth shut, knowing that anything she said would either come out as an excuse or sound defensive.

"Your father thinks it's a great idea," Ashleigh added. "I have my doubts, but Star is your horse and the choice is yours."

Christina took a deep breath and stared at her

mother. "I think it's a good idea," she finally said, dreading the expression she was sure she'd see on Ashleigh's face.

But Ashleigh looked as though she had expected Christina's answer, and she nodded. "You can take him over there this evening," she said. "I'll help you get Star's equipment loaded in the trailer. It will only be until we head for Pimlico," she reminded Christina.

Christina nodded, silent, then turned toward the barn. She felt as though a huge weight had just been lifted from her shoulders, and now she had a lot of things to pack—for the colt and for herself.

7

"THE PREAKNESS IS LOOKING PRETTY GOOD FOR GRATIS
and me," Wolf said as he and Christina jogged Star and
Gratis around the Tall Oaks track. In the faint early
morning light, Christina couldn't see the other
jockey's face clearly when she glanced in his direction.

"It's good to be confident, but there are no sure
races," she said as she balanced in the stirrups, paying
close attention to her colt's steady gait. Star trotted
smoothly, his chin tucked and his strides long. Christina was pleased with the way Star was moving, energetic and focused. If he was this way on the track, the
Preakness would look pretty good for Star, too.

"I realize there aren't any sure races," Wolf replied.
"You and Star proved that."

Christina narrowed her eyes in his direction, but Wolf was looking straight ahead, not paying any attention to her reaction.

"But," he continued, "with Image not racing, the only other horse that came in ahead of us is Celtic Mist."

"So?" Christina didn't remind Wolf that Star wasn't going to end up dead last two races in a row. If the other jockey was overconfident, that would be his problem, not hers.

"I heard something about that Townsend Acres jockey, Emilio Casados," Wolf said. "You can't tell anyone else, though."

"What did you hear?" Christina's curiosity was piqued.

"He broke his knee a couple of years ago," Wolf said. "If you watch the videos of his races, he always puts his weight on his right knee and positions himself to protect his left one. If you get to the inside, he's going to be worried about reinjuring himself, and that could hurt his race."

"Oh," Christina said. "That sounds really sporting."

"A million-dollar purse is serious competition, Chris," Wolf said abruptly. "Sporting has nothing to do with it. Besides," he added, "the Townsends haven't exactly treated you fairly. Cindy told me how Brad tried to force you to give up Star. Why would you worry about having a little edge on his jockey?"

Christina shrugged. Wolf had a point. She'd just never thought about racing that way.

"Okay, you two," Cindy called from the rail. The riders slowed their horses and circled back to where Cindy waited for them at the edge of the track. She looked over the numbers on her clipboard, then smiled at Christina. "You need to walk Star out and put him up. Wolf," she said, turning to her own jockey, "you and Gratis need to do a mile gallop, then you can cool him out."

"Star could use a gallop, too," Christina said, but Cindy shook her head.

"I worked out a schedule for his works with your mom," she said. "Star gallops tomorrow, not today."

Christina nodded. Cindy and Ashleigh had spent a lot of time deciding what Star's best training program would be for the next several days, and Christina wasn't going to argue. She walked Star off the track and untacked him, then threw his cooling sheet over his sweaty back.

"Let's go for a walk, fellow," she said. She led the colt up the tractor rows between the large paddocks surrounding the Tall Oaks barns. The sun was coming up, a bright orange ball low on the horizon, and the mist curling from the ground gave the surroundings a mysterious feel. The birds were beginning to awaken, and their cheerful singing made Christina smile. She patted Star's neck as they strolled toward a copse of woods on the edge of the paddocks. "This is such a nice place," she told the colt.

Star pricked his ears as they neared the woods and picked up his pace, tugging at the lead.

"You want to go for a hack, don't you?" Christina said. She nodded. "Me too. But I don't think we'll be allowed to do any fun riding until after the Triple Crown." She sighed. "Maybe we can get Cindy to take one of her saddle horses and at least go for a short trail ride. That might just do us both some good."

After they returned to the barn, she gave the colt a thorough grooming, then went looking for Cindy to ask about going on a ride later.

"She's in her office," Beckie, the Australian groom, informed Christina. "Is there anything you need me to do for Star today while you're at school?"

"Just keep an eye on him," Christina said, smiling at the friendly groom. "He likes a bit of carrot once in a while, too."

"Great," Beckie said. "I just happen to keep a few pieces in my pocket for horses like him."

Christina headed for Cindy's office but stopped outside when she saw Ben standing near Cindy's desk.

"When Gratis wins the Preakness," she heard Cindy say, "we'll be able to draw some good outside mares for breeding. I just hope Wolf doesn't blow it with his lack of experience."

"Who else could you get to ride the colt?" Ben asked. "Christina will be racing Star, and Melanie is still recovering from her broken rib. We already went through every available jockey in Kentucky. Not one of them could manage your cranky colt."

"I know," Cindy said. "Let's just hope Wolf can handle the race."

Instead of walking in, Christina turned away. She thought about Cindy having her cool Star out without a long work, taking it easy on the colt. According to Cindy, those were Ashleigh's orders, but keeping Star in top condition wasn't Cindy's concern. Christina walked down the aisle toward Star's stall, feeling once again as though she were all alone.

The school day passed slowly, with Christina's thoughts on Star. When she got a test back from her biology teacher, she stared at the grade in disbelief.

"What's wrong with you?"

97

She glanced up at the girl sitting next to her. Andrea Jackson, a good friend of Katie Garrity's, was staring at her. Christina didn't know Andrea well. She was in the drama club with Katie and they'd eaten lunch at the same table a few times, but Andrea wasn't a horse person. Christina realized the only people she was close to were involved in riding and racing as much as she was.

She smiled weakly. "I got a D," she admitted.

Andrea raised her eyebrows. "Christina Reese, honor student extraordinaire, got a lousy grade on a test?" Andrea held up her own paper with a red B scrawled across the top. "I had to work my fingers off for this grade," she said proudly.

"I've been a little busy," Christina said defensively.

"I didn't say you weren't," Andrea said. "I was just surprised. You do so much else, I didn't think you ever had to study." She offered Christina a friendly smile. "I wish I were as smart as you are."

Christina stared at the other girl, stunned. Did people think she was just lucky, that she didn't have to work for her grades? Didn't they know how much time she put into her schoolwork?

She returned to Tall Oaks after school, still thinking about Andrea's comments. She changed in the spare room in Cindy's cottage, where she was staying, and went out to Star's new turnout. "People must think I'm the most spoiled brat in the world," she told the colt as she slipped his halter on. Star nudged her, demanding a pet, and she rubbed her hand over the white swirl on his forehead. "I'm not spoiled," she said. "Am I?" But when she thought about it, she wasn't so sure. Not too many girls her age had the opportunities that she'd been given. *But*, she told herself, *it isn't like I live the perfect life. I do work hard for what I have.*

After grooming Star thoroughly and wrapping his legs carefully, she saddled the colt.

"Where are you headed?" Cindy asked, walking out of her office.

"I was going to take Star for a quick ride," Christina said, buckling the girth. She didn't want to ask Cindy to go with her now, after overhearing the trainer's conversation with Gratis's owner. *You're being silly*, she chided herself. *Cindy isn't trying to hurt Star's changes in the race. She just wants to see her horse succeed.*

"You shouldn't go alone," Cindy said.

"Star and I will be fine," Christina replied.

Cindy nodded. "I'm sure you would be," she said. "But if you can hang on a few minutes, I'll throw a saddle on one of the Arabians and go with you."

"Do you have time?" Christina asked, surprised. "I

thought you were busy perfecting your plans for Gratis and shopping for broodmares."

Cindy grinned. "I've dragged Ben to five farms in two days," she said. "I've got the names of seven fillies I want to buy at the Keeneland auction. With some luck we'll be able to pick up one or two of them, so that's done. As far as Gratis goes," she continued, "I was pleased beyond words to see him place so well in the Derby. But really, Chris, just racing him in the Triple Crown series is good publicity for the farm. I never had any expectations that he'd do as well as he did."

Christina felt her jaw drop slightly. "But you talk like you expect him to win the Preakness," she said.

"Yeah," Cindy replied, looking amused. "I couldn't enter him without thinking the best, Chris. Now hold up, and I'll saddle Dove so we can go for a little trail ride."

Cindy hurried off, returning a few minutes later with a small gray mare on a lead. Ben had purchased the mare, an easygoing veteran of a therapeutic riding program, so that Cindy could ride in spite of her bad shoulder.

Soon they were both in the saddle, walking along the tractor lane. Cindy looked across the empty paddocks. "In another couple of years they'll be full of mares with Champion's and Gratis's foals at their sides," she said dreamily. "Working with Ben to make this a great farm is like a dream come true for me."

Christina looked across the gently rolling pastures and nodded. "You're lucky," she said. "I wish I knew how to make my dreams come true." She thought of Parker, going after Olympic gold while she was chasing the Triple Crown. She had assumed they would always be close, with their shared passion for horses to keep them together. But they were moving in such opposite directions that it seemed their paths would never cross again.

They reached a path leading into the woods, and with Dove in the lead, the horses walked along the shady trail. Star sighed deeply and pushed his nose toward a clump of brush. When a squirrel scolded at them, the colt pricked his ears and raised his head, looking around curiously. Christina patted his neck.

"Have you ever heard the old saying 'Be careful what you wish for'?" Cindy asked, twisting in the saddle so that she could see Christina. Dove continued on steadily, not needing a lot of control as she ambled down the dirt path.

"What do you mean?" Christina asked.

"I never thought beyond becoming a jockey and racing," Cindy said. "It's a hard life, Chris. A lot harder than I ever thought it would be."

Christina stared at Cindy, confused. "But you had a great life in New York," she said. "You made being a jockey seem so exciting."

Cindy nodded. "It can be," she said. "There's nothing I'd rather be doing. But you're living at home, Chris, with your family around you and your own horses to ride. If you get out on your own, it can be really lonely. You have to watch your weight constantly, and if you make a mistake on the track, no one forgets it. And if you're injured," she continued, tilting her head toward her left shoulder, "the trainers and owners you thought liked you don't want anything to do with you." She sighed and slowed Dove as the trail widened so that Star and the mare could walk side by side.

"But look at what you've done," Christina argued. "You spent years doing what you love, and now you're training and working with Ben at Tall Oaks. Didn't you get what you wished for?"

Cindy nodded slowly as they turned the horses to return to the barn. "But there are no guarantees and no sure things," she said. "Right up to finding a jockey for Gratis and fighting Brad for Champion's ownership." She sighed deeply, then patted Dove's neck. "And by doing what I loved for so long, I almost wasn't able to ride ever again." Dove tossed her head, flipping her silky mane, and Cindy ran her hand along the mare's crest, smoothing the hair back into place. "It hasn't been all fun and excitement."

"What would you have done differently?" Christina demanded, trying to imagine Cindy anywhere but around horses.

"I would have spent some of my money going to college," Cindy said firmly.

Christina settled her weight into the saddle. "College," she repeated. "What for?"

"I would have a degree in business management by now," Cindy said. "I would be more of a help to Tall Oaks than just a horse trainer. In fact," she said, "I'm going to start taking classes this fall at the community college. It took me a long time to realize an education won't hurt me." She grinned at Christina.

"You're going to college?" Christina said, trying to picture Cindy sitting in a classroom.

Cindy nodded firmly. "That's right," she said. "I should have done it a long time ago, but it's never too late."

While she groomed Star, carefully wiping his delicate legs down with liniment, her conversation with Cindy kept running through her head. Maybe deciding not to go on to college wasn't the best plan in the world. But she was so busy, and so tired of going to class every day, that she couldn't imagine making time for college after the summer. She had too many other things she wanted to do first.

The next morning, Wolf was already on the track when Christina brought Star out of the barn. She held her colt by the rail, watching Wolf jog the big bay counterclockwise along the outside rail, holding his pace down. Gratis moved smartly, his strides long and elegant. Wolf sat lightly in the saddle, looking more like he were riding an old school horse than balancing on the back of a powerful racehorse. As Christina watched, Wolf turned Gratis and pushed him into a gallop, moving to the inside rail. He rose in the stirrups and tightened the reins, pumping his hands in time to the movements of Gratis's head. The jockey looked confident and professional, and Christina felt herself tense. Beside her Star snorted softly and struck at the ground, his shod hoof making a metallic sound when it hit.

"Let's get out there, boy," she murmured, collecting Star's reins. "We need to show Wolf we can ride as well as he does."

She warmed Star up by massaging his legs and gently stretching them, loosening the muscles and warming them up. Then she swung onto the colt's back and walked him onto the track.

When she turned him so that he was moving opposite the direction he would be if he were racing, she walked him briskly for one circuit of the track, then pushed him into a slow jog.

"Hurry up!" Wolf hollered as he galloped by on Gratis. "You slackers are missing the best part of the day!"

Christina felt a bit of annoyance. Wolf was out of school. Working full time at Tall Oaks, he had little else to do besides handle the horses and ride. She envied him the time he had to spend with the animals. It was fine for Cindy to announce that she was going back to college, but Christina wondered how Cindy would feel about school once the homework started piling up and she still had dozens of other things to take care of.

Finally Star was ready to work, and she turned him, pushing him into a smooth canter. When Wolf and Gratis passed them, Star snorted loudly and tossed his head, nearly yanking the reins from her hands. Christina settled her weight firmly on his back as he fought her.

"Settle down," she scolded him as he pranced sideways, trying to pick up his speed so he could catch up with the other colt. "This is a workout, not a race."

When Wolf caught up with them on his next round of the track, he slowed Gratis to keep pace with Star. "I think Cindy wants to breeze them both today," he informed her.

Christina nodded. "She told me." Star was demanding all her attention, and a little smile of satisfaction tugged at her mouth. The previous day's little hack had given the colt a fresh attitude. She patted his neck. "We'll take another trail ride before we go up to Pimlico," she promised the colt. "I think it gave us both a change of scenery that we needed."

At Cindy's signal, the jockeys came around the curve of the track together and pushed their colts into top speed. Christina watched as the first pole flashed by, then focused her attention between Star's ears, the ground beneath them blurring as the colt picked up speed.

She sensed more than felt a touch as Gratis crowded close to them. Star faltered a little, losing his pace, and Gratis charged ahead, sweeping past the pole marking the four-furlong breeze well ahead of Star.

Christina was seething as she slowed Star and turned him, holding the colt to a steady jog as he wound down after the run.

When Wolf and Gratis came up beside them,

Christina glared at the other jockey. "What was that?" she demanded. "You bumped us!"

"I never touched you," Wolf said. "We were close beside you, but Gratis never touched Star. You flinched and slowed your colt. That was a lousy bit of riding on your part." He offered her a cocky grin. "Ride like that, and Gratis and I won't have any competition in the Preakness."

With that, he urged Gratis into a faster jog. Christina slowed Star to a walk, staring at Wolf's back as he rode away. Was he right? Had she reacted to how close the horses were? There wasn't any way to tell. And if he hadn't done anything illegal, he would have won the race. She slipped from Star's back, troubled by the thought. Maybe she was too cautious, babying Star on the track and not taking the chances that could win them at least one of the jewels of the Triple Crown.

"We'll see," she murmured to Star as she slipped his saddle from his back. "I know you can handle it, so maybe I need to be a little more aggressive." She sighed as she buckled his cooling sheet into place. The question was, could she do it?

8

"I CAN'T BELIEVE HOW MANY PEOPLE AND HORSES ARE HERE already," Dani exclaimed in greeting as Christina climbed from the cab of the Whitebrook pickup Wednesday morning. Dani parked a wheelbarrow near the front of the horse trailer. "You'd think the Preakness was running tomorrow, not Saturday!"

The parking area behind Maryland's Pimlico racetrack was filled with vans and horse trailers, and it had taken Joe several minutes to find a spot to park the Whitebrook rig. All around them, handlers were unloading horses and leading them toward the backside.

"It's going to be a busy week," Christina said, walking toward the back of the pickup. The trailer rocked as Star shifted his weight, impatient to get out after the long drive from Lexington to Baltimore.

"Hold on, boy," Christina called. "We'll have you out in just a minute."

"Star's stall is all ready for him," Dani informed her as she opened the door to the trailer's tack room and began unloading equipment into the wheelbarrow. "Cindy and Gratis are already here, and that Celtic Meadows horse, Wild 'n' Free, is on the track now. He looks really good, Chris."

Christina acknowledged Dani's comment with a tight-lipped smile. "I'm sure he does," she said, trying not to think about how the Preakness was going to turn out. She was eager to see how the other horses looked so that she could size up the competition, but first she wanted to get Star settled and start working him on the Pimlico track. He might not have been too exciting to watch in the Derby, but she knew what kind of power her colt had. Star could be just as intimidating as any of the other world-class Thoroughbreds running. More than anything, she wanted to show the racing fans that Star's loss in the Derby was nothing more than a fluke.

Joe came around to the back of the trailer, rubbing his back. "I'm getting too old for these long drives," he commented, grinning at Dani and Christina. "It feels good to get out and stretch." The trailer rocked again as Star stomped his foot impatiently. "Let's get Star out of there," he said, unlatching the tailgate. "I'm sure he could use a good stretch, too."

Christina climbed inside and released the trailer ties, then backed Star outside. Star looked around, raised his head, and tested the air, then emitted a loud whinny. Several horses answered his call, making Joe chuckle. "He's telling them to watch out because Wonder's Star is here," Joe said. He patted the colt's glistening red-brown shoulder. "And you are going to burn up the track, aren't you, fellow?"

"Of course he is," Dani said. "Star is going to rock out there."

Joe stayed behind to lock up the truck and trailer while Dani led the way toward the rows of stalls, pushing the loaded wheelbarrow. "When are your parents coming up?" she asked Christina.

"They'll be here tomorrow," Christina said. *Much to my relief,* she thought. *I don't need more pressure from Mom right now.*

The backside at Pimlico was a swarm of horses, jockeys, trainers, and owners. Christina saw several people she knew as she led Star down the aisle to Whitebrook's assigned stall.

"Hey, Chris!" Vicky Frontiere called. She was

standing with two other jockeys, and Christina waved at her.

"The odds on that Whitebrook colt are lousy," one of the other jockeys commented in a low voice. "That colt is the long shot right now."

Christina tugged Star's lead, hurrying him along. She wasn't going to listen to the track talk. She and Star were going to race to win, and that was the only thing that mattered at the moment.

"Can you believe all these people?" Dani asked, swiveling her head from side to side. "It looks like everyone on the East Coast is here already."

Christina nodded, her attention on Star and getting him through the crowded aisle. "I know," she said. "And it's only going to get more overwhelming."

When they reached Star's stall, Dani opened the door. "I think you'll approve, Star," she said, looking at the colt. "I put down a nice thick layer of bedding for you and made sure your water bucket was filled." She stepped back and made a sweeping motion with her arm. "I hope you find your accommodations satisfactory, sir."

Christina couldn't help but chuckle as she led the colt into the spacious stall. "Star's going to believe he's royalty," she said to the groom as Dani latched the door behind them.

"He is," Dani said firmly, resting her forearms on top of the stall door. "He may not be able to get all the jewels in the Triple Crown, but two out of three will still be great."

Christina flashed a smile at the groom. "Thanks for the vote of confidence," she said. "We need it, don't we, Star?" she asked the colt, who was busy checking out his new home. He sniffed at the strange walls, then dropped his nose to smell the bedding before he stuck his nose into the water bucket to inspect the contents. He raised his head, water dribbling from his lips.

"I think he approves," Christina said.

"Then I'll go unload this stuff in the tack room," Dani said, nodding toward the loaded wheelbarrow. "I'll see you in a little while."

After Dani left, Christina slipped Star's halter off and stepped outside the stall. The colt hung his head over the half door, and Christina stroked his nose thoughtfully. "This is pretty exciting, isn't it, boy?" she murmured, watching grooms leading the other lean Thoroughbreds to their stalls.

She saw Cindy McLean winding her way between the grooms and trainers talking in the aisle, and she waved at the petite blonde.

"How's your boy?" Cindy asked when she reached

them. She gave Star's nose a pet. "Did he make the trip okay?"

"He's fine," Christina said. "Star travels really well."

"We'll put him and Gratis on the track first thing tomorrow morning," Cindy said. "They'll both get a good feel for the track footing."

Joe walked up, a folding chair and a magazine in his hands. "If you two want to check out the other horses, I'll keep an eye on Star," he offered.

"Thanks," Christina replied. She gave Star a kiss on the nose, then she and Cindy started along the aisle.

"There's Speed.com," Cindy said, pointing across the wide row between the stalls.

The colt had his back to the door, and all Christina could see in the dim interior of the stall was Speed.com's muscular rump. "And there's Alexis," she said as the colt's trainer strode up the aisle. "Yuck."

As the farm manager at Tall Oaks, Alexis had used her position to buy and sell horses at a profit to herself, pilfering large sums of money from the farm's previous owner, Fredericka Graber. When her unscrupulous scheme was uncovered, Alexis had disappeared, only to reappear on the racing scene as Speed.com's trainer.

113

"She isn't exactly a reputable character," Cindy said. "I'm surprised Dustin Gates hired her. You'd think someone who owns and runs a huge corporation would have done some serious background checks before handing his racehorse over to someone like Alexis."

Christina nodded. "I guess he isn't a serious horse person," she pointed out. "Alexis could have told him anything about her experiences with racing and he wouldn't have known any better. Besides," she added, "Alexis does know good horses."

"That's true," Cindy said. "She managed to unload Fredericka's best at a tidy profit before her little operation was exposed."

They hurried past Speed.com's stall, avoiding Alexis, who slipped into her colt's stall without noticing them.

"I see TV Time," Christina said as they turned to walk down another row of stalls. "I was surprised that Vicky is going to race him again."

Cindy nodded. "I talked to her this morning," she said. "She doesn't have a lot of hope for winning, but still, racing in the Preakness is quite an honor, no matter what."

"Celtic Meadows' stalls are over here," Christina said, pointing out a large banner. "I want to see Wild 'n' Free." The colt's stall was empty, and after checking

114

out some of the other Preakness hopefuls, Cindy and Christina headed for the track, where a few horses were still being worked in the late morning hours.

When they reached the track, Christina saw Vince Jones standing near the rail, his attention on a colt galloping along the inside rail.

She heard Cindy gasp, and when she shifted her attention from the trainer to the running horse, she understood why.

"That colt is Affirmed all over again," Cindy said, sounding awed.

They walked closer to the rail, Christina's attention locked on the chestnut colt as he swept around the curve of the track.

"It's been a few years since I saw you," a strange voice said, and Christina turned to see a man walking up to them. There was a young woman with him, tall and slender, with long dark hair and a T-shirt that had the name CELTIC MEADOWS printed across the front. *She must be a groom for Wild 'n' Free*, Christina thought, wondering if Ghyllian Hollis, the farm owner, was at the track. Probably not, she decided. Most of the owners didn't show up until race day, with all the excitement and publicity that came with it.

"Steve Cauthen," Cindy said, extending her hand. "It's good to see you."

Christina stared at the jockey. Steve had been only eighteen when he rode Affirmed to Triple Crown victory. Christina had watched tapes of the races several times, always amazed at the skill Steve had displayed in working with Affirmed.

Steve smiled warmly at Cindy. "It's great to see you, too," he said. "And it's nice to be back in the States. I had some good years in England, but there's really no place like home." He turned to the woman standing next to him. "Ghyllian, this is Cindy McLean. We raced against each other a few times at Belmont. The track lost a great jockey when Cindy had to retire last year."

He looked closely at Christina. "We haven't actually met before," he said, "but I've been following you and Wonder's Star since you brought him onto the track. That colt of yours has a lot of potential. You had a bad break in the Derby, but I'm sure you'll pull it together for the Preakness."

"I hope so," Christina said, feeling a little overwhelmed to have one of the greatest jockeys of all time offering her words of encouragement.

"It's a pleasure to meet you," Ghyllian broke in, and Christina turned her attention to the woman, who appeared to be close to Cindy's age, in her early thirties.

"My father and I followed Wonder's career

closely," she told Christina. "We loved to watch her run. It must be pretty special for you to be racing her last foal."

"It is," Christina said, then glanced at the track, where the exercise rider was bringing Wild 'n' Free to the rail. Vince Jones was leaning forward, but they were too far away to hear what he was telling the rider.

"He's got quite a presence, doesn't he?" Steve said, sounding a little wistful as he gazed at Wild 'n' Free. "It makes me think I'm seeing my old friend Affirmed again."

Christina watched the rider hop from the colt's back and lead the horse toward the backside, and Vince Jones turned and strode over to them.

"Good to see you," he said, giving her shoulder a hearty squeeze. He extended a hand to Cindy. "How's Gratis doing?" he asked. "I have to tell you, I don't miss working with that monster."

Cindy laughed. "But Vince," she said, "he's a magnificent horse."

"He's a pain in the neck," Vince said gruffly, then turned to Ghyllian. "Christina here was the only jockey on the track who could work with that beast," he said. "You should see this girl ride."

Christina gaped at Vince. When she had worked for the trainer, he had expressed nothing but criticism of her riding, no matter how hard she tried or how well she did. But she had to admit that Vince's pushing and prodding had helped her improve her racing skills, and she appreciated what he had done for her.

"Since when did you start cloning racehorses?" Cindy asked Vince in a teasing voice.

The trainer shook his head. "I couldn't believe it the first time I saw Wild 'n' Free," he said. "When Steve told me the colt looked like Affirmed all over again, I thought he was just trying to get me to agree to train for Celtic Meadows. But when I saw that colt, I was stunned."

"Isn't he amazing?" Ghyllian asked. "We couldn't believe it when he outgrew his gangly stage and matured into Affirmed's twin."

"Where have you been hiding him?" Cindy asked.

"We were training him in Ireland," Ghyllian said. "We never dreamed he'd be Triple Crown material, but when Steve was visiting our facility in Shannon, he pushed us to bring Wild 'n' Free here to race in the Derby."

"What happened?" Christina asked. "He wasn't entered in the race."

"We missed some deadlines and had some problems with Free's trainer," Ghyllian explained. She gestured at Steve Cauthen. "Lucky for the farm, Steve made some contacts for us, and here we are, gearing up for the Preakness."

"Are you named in any races today?" Vince asked Christina. "Another one of Celtic Meadows' horses is running in the fifth race, and the jockey is out sick. Would you be interested?"

"I'd love to," Christina said promptly, then hesitated. "Uh, this colt isn't another Gratis, is he?"

Vince chuckled and shook his head. "Actually, it's a filly. Ghyllian's Junebug. This is her first race, and I can't think of a better jockey than you to ride her."

"I'll do it," Christina said. Before long, she was in the jockey's lounge, weighing in. She pulled the Celtic Meadows' racing shirt, with its dark green shamrocks scattered over a white background, over her head and tucked it into her nylon breeches. Once she was dressed, her long hair plaited into a tight braid and pinned at the nape of her neck, she left the dressing room and returned to the lounge.

She saw Wolf sitting at a table with some other riders, playing cards. He didn't notice her, and she didn't see any other jockeys she wanted to talk to, so she settled into an easy chair and watched the preparations for the first race. When she looked around, Wolf was gone. She turned back to the television in time to see a shot of the viewing paddock. Wolf was being given a leg up onto a rangy bay colt, and Christina leaned forward to observe the other jockey's ride.

The colt loaded into the number three position, and Christina watched closely, waiting for the start of the race.

When the horses came out with the sound of the starting bell, the number three horse hit the track with a surge of power. The horses to the left veered toward the inside, but to Christina's surprise, Wolf held his ground, riding straight, so the horses to his right were forced to keep toward the outside rail. It wasn't until they were nearly to the turn that Wolf moved to the inside, his horse keeping pace with the lead horse.

Christina watched Wolf move so close to the lead horse that she was sure they were going to collide, but at the last second she saw the young jockey bring his whip down onto his horse's hip. The bay stretched his legs and charged forward, passing the lead horse in just a few strides.

When Wolf came across the finish line in first place, Christina was impressed. He had calculated the race well, and even though his racing style didn't seem quite right, he had won. Maybe she needed to ride more like Wolf.

"That kid is going to get himself into trouble," she heard one of the older jockeys comment.

"No kidding," another voice chimed in. "If he were riding next to me, I might be tempted to give him a little lesson in fair racing."

"You mean like accidentally hitting his foot with your whip?" another jockey said with a laugh. "I know a few jocks who've broken a toe or two before they figured out that they needed to clean up their act."

Christina inhaled sharply, but she kept her mouth shut. She debated whether she should tell Wolf what the other riders were saying, but she wasn't sure he would listen. And she was certain he wouldn't change his riding style just because it annoyed the other jockeys.

As the third race started, Christina headed for the saddling area with the other jockeys who were riding in the fifth race. Some of the riders talked and joked with each other, but Christina kept to herself, sorting out in her mind how she would ride the race.

It wasn't uncommon for a jockey to be named on a horse she or he had never seen before, meeting the animal in the viewing paddock, but Christina preferred to spend time with the horses she rode, getting to know them before she took them onto the track. *This is a good experience for me,* she told herself, feeling a tense knot form in her stomach.

When she reached the viewing paddock, Ghyllian

was standing at the number four spot, waiting for her. The owner had changed into a green sundress, and her long hair was pinned up, making her look a little more like an affluent horse owner than a stable hand.

She smiled at Christina. "My colors look good on you," she said. "I'm looking forward to seeing you race Junebug. She's a real sweet horse. I'm sure you'll like her."

"I hope we can do a good job for you," Christina replied, glancing over at the saddling area to check out her ride. A bay filly was wearing the number four blanket, Christina's tiny racing saddle on her back. The filly looked alert and energetic, but when the race-horses were led around the viewing paddock, Christina realized the competition was going to be tough.

"Vince said to tell you just keep to the inside and keep her rated until the last two furlongs," Ghyllian said. "It should be a good race for both of you."

"Got it." Christina stepped close to Junebug as the handler slowed the prancing filly in front of them. Christina settled onto the saddle, and in a minute they were on the track for the post parade.

Once they were in the gate, Christina rose over the filly's shoulders, braced for the start. When the gate sprang open, Junebug leaped forward and they surged onto the track, the filly veering toward the rail with the rest of the pack.

"So far, so good," Christina murmured to the galloping filly. Junebug flicked her ears back at the sound of Christina's voice. Encouraged by the filly's response, Christina leaned forward. "Come on, girl," she urged, kneading her hands up Junebug's neck. One of the fillies ahead of them went wide, and Christina could see clear track ahead of them. She steered her racehorse into the hole, but to her right, a big black filly darted around them, blocking their way as the jockey drove his horse into the opening.

Determined to move her filly into a good position, Christina took Junebug wide, but with the short race and strong-running fillies ahead of them, Junebug didn't have a chance to close the distance. As they reached the end of the six-furlong race, Junebug was in fifth place. Christina hopped off the sweating filly, disappointed with herself.

"You did fine," Vince told her when she walked off the track. "That race was a good experience for her."

And a bad one for me, Christina thought, heading back toward the jockeys' lounge. When she walked into the lounge, Wolf was sitting in one of the easy chairs, drinking a can of cola. He raised it to her in a mock toast, then rose and crossed the room to greet her.

"I watched your race," he said. "You know, if you had been a little less timid, that filly could have won. But you waited too long to go for that gap." He shook his head. "I'm telling you, Chris, you need to quit being so cautious."

"Thanks for the advice," Christina said, then hurried toward the locker room. *Where does an apprentice jockey get off telling me how to race?* she fumed silently as she stripped off her racing silks. But Wolf had won his race that day, and even with a good horse under her, she had blown it. She had three days until the Preakness, and she didn't have much hope of doing any better than she had in the Derby. *Poor Star*, she thought. *After all he's gone through, he's stuck with me for a jockey. And I know he deserves much better.*

9

THE TRACK WAS ILLUMINATED BY VAPOR LIGHTS WHEN Christina walked Star out to the rail on Thursday morning. Another rider was standing by the track, and she nodded in greeting as she led Star past him. Cindy was waiting for her near the gap in the rail.

"Beckie should be here with Gratis any minute," Cindy said. "I haven't seen Wolf yet. You can go ahead and start warming Star up."

She gave Christina a leg up onto Star's tall back. Christina rode the colt onto the track and began walking him along the outside rail. The colt danced beneath her, and Christina tightened the reins. "Knock it off," she said in a firm voice. "You'll get a chance to gallop a little this morning, but let's get used to the track first."

125

Star quickly settled into a strong walk, and after they had circled the track once, Cindy had her move him into an easy jog. Star seemed to like the track footing, and he moved lightly on the loam surface. Christina patted his neck. "You're in the best shape ever," she told the colt. "We're going to have a good race on Saturday, aren't we?"

Star tossed his head a little, and Christina nodded. "You think so, too—I can tell." She had the colt speed up a little. "You run your best for me, don't you, boy?" she asked. "I promise, Star, I'll make sure you get every chance to finish in front."

By the time Star was thoroughly warm, the sky was beginning to lighten. From the far side of the track, Christina saw Wolf astride Gratis. Cindy was talking to him, and the jockey was nodding as though he was agreeing with whatever she was saying.

Suddenly Star flung his head up and began to prance, swinging his hindquarters sideways. Christina brought him back under control and glanced over her shoulder. A massive bay colt was jogging up behind them. As he drew near, Christina saw that his rider was the jockey she had seen earlier.

They trotted by, and Christina watched the colt move out smartly. "Wow," she murmured. "That is one powerful-looking Thoroughbred." She had never seen the horse before, all sleek muscles and solid-looking legs. "I'm glad he's not running in the Preakness," she told Star. "That colt looks dangerous to me."

She brought Star to a stop when they reached Cindy. "Now what?" she asked, feeling the heat coming off of Star's neck.

"Gallop him a half mile, then we're going to breeze him," Cindy directed her. "Let's do a little blowout to clear his pipes, then cool him out. That'll be his last work until the race."

Christina nodded and turned Star, who arched his neck and pricked his ears when they changed direction on the track. Christina chuckled. "This is the right way to be going, isn't it, boy?" she asked, giving the colt some rein. Star broke into an eager gallop, and Christina balanced in her stirrups, keeping her weight off Star's back as they ran easily along the inner track rail.

She realized she hadn't asked Cindy about the bay colt, who was finishing his warm-up as she galloped Star past the poles marking the furlongs. When they neared the pole where Cindy would start her stopwatch, Christina leaned forward and collected her reins. Star responded to her position change and broke into a hard gallop, stretching his long legs as they raced along the straight stretch. Christina felt the

127

power in his strides, and a surge of excitement ran through her.

"That's my boy," she exclaimed as they shot past the fourth pole and she started to bring the colt around. "You are more than ready to run Saturday. I can feel it."

She walked the colt back to where Cindy was discussing Gratis's work with Wolf. Cindy glanced at her. "Excellent fractions," the trainer said, smiling. "You can get him off the track and cooled out now."

She turned back to Wolf and propped her fisted hands on her hips. "I don't want to see you use that kind of move," she began. As she lectured the young jockey, Christina hopped from Star's back and led her colt away. Star needed to be pampered and taken care of, and that was much more important than hearing Cindy getting after Wolf for something he had done with Gratis.

As they neared the end of the track, Christina heard the thundering of hooves, and she turned to see the bay colt galloping along the inside rail. She froze in her tracks as the powerful colt raced toward them, his long legs devouring a hunk of track with each stride. "Holy cow," she muttered as the jockey slowed him before they reached the curve. "Who is that?" But there was no one around to answer her.

Dani was waiting for her with Star's cooling sheet, and they quickly untacked the sweaty colt and buckled his cover into place. "I'll walk him out," Christina said, patting Star's neck.

"Then I'll go clean this stuff up," Dani replied, draping the saddle across her forearm.

Christina led Star to the open area behind the shed rows and began walking him steadily, checking frequently to see how his temperature and heart rate were. It didn't take long for the colt to recover from the short workout, and Christina led him to the wash rack and clipped his lead to the crossties.

Star enjoyed the leisurely bath, craning his neck to the side as she scrubbed his coat with a soapy brush. "You *are* spoiled," she laughed, massaging his neck with thick lather. "And you deserve it," she added. She finished bathing the colt, then blanketed him again and walked him back to his stall. Dani had replaced the bedding and filled Star's hay net. As soon as Christina closed the stall door, the colt grabbed a mouthful from the net and began munching contently.

"Christina!"

She looked away from the colt to see her parents walking toward the stall, Melanie at their side. Christina did a double take when she saw her cousin.

Ashleigh gave her a quick hug, then looked into

Star's stall. "You both look pretty comfortable," she commented. "We saw Cindy on our way in. She was really pleased with Star's times this morning. Saturday should be a good day for both of you."

Christina nodded. "Star really seems to like this track," she said.

"That's good to hear," Ashleigh replied. "If you don't need anything, your father and I are going to head over to the track kitchen. I could use a cup of coffee." Her parents walked away, and Christina wondered how long it would be before they heard about her race the day before. Ashleigh hadn't wanted her to ride before the Preakness, and the loss on Ghyllian Hollis's filly would only give her a chance to point out that she'd been right.

"How did Mom and Dad manage to drag you away from Townsend Acres?" she asked Melanie. "They must have done some serious talking to get you to leave Image."

"I asked them for a ride up here," Melanie said. "I've been cleared to start riding again."

"That's wonderful," Christina said, surprised to hear that Melanie was going to be allowed back on the track so soon after the Derby. "But I thought they would make you wait a few more weeks with that broken rib."

Melanie shook her head firmly. "I can't start racing for another week or so, but I'm okayed to exercise-ride for now."

"So that doesn't explain why you left Image to come to Pimlico," Christina said.

"I came up here to help with Celtic Mist," Melanie said. "Brad asked me to." She raised her hand in a silencing gesture when Christina started to open her mouth. "I hated to leave Image, but I could hardly tell him no." She sighed.

"I'm sure they'll take excellent care of Image for you," Christina reassured her.

Just then Dani returned to the stall, pushing the empty wheelbarrow. She greeted Melanie, then settled in a chair near Star's door. "I'll be here if you want to go get some breakfast," she told Christina.

"Good idea," Christina said, pressing her hand to her stomach. "I forgot all about eating until you said something."

When they got to the track kitchen, located behind the grandstand, Christina saw her parents at a table with some people she didn't know. Since it was too late for breakfast, she and Melanie ordered hamburgers and sat down.

"There's Ghyllian Hollis," Melanie said, pointing across the room.

Christina saw the Celtic Meadows owner at a table with Vince Jones, and she looked back at Melanie. "When did you meet her?" she asked.

"She was at Brad's to see the therapy pool," Melanie said. "She's the one who sold Celtic Mist to him."

"I wonder why she sold him," Christina mused. "He's a good horse."

Melanie nodded. "She told me she was so invested in Wild 'n' Free that she had to decide between him and Celtic Mist. I offered to work some of her horses for her," she continued. "She has some other good stock she's getting ready to race."

"That would be great," Christina said. It seemed to her that anything would be better than seeing Melanie spend all her time at Townsend Acres.

"Celtic Mist's odds are at two to one," Melanie commented, biting into a french fry. "People are saying he's a sure thing for the Preakness."

Christina looked at her cousin, surprised, and quickly took a bite of burger so that she wouldn't have to respond to Melanie's comment. She was tempted to ask whom Melanie had been talking to. Since she was living at Townsend Acres and indebted to Brad, chances were good that she was only repeating what he had said about the horse.

"I'm sure it will be a great race," she said, pushing her plate away, her appetite gone.

The girls headed back to the shed rows, detouring behind the stalls to look at the horses being cooled out on the mechanical walkers.

"Look at that colt," Christina said, pointing at the powerful bay she had seen on the track earlier. The racehorse's hindquarters rippled with muscles, and he walked with an easy grace that hinted of his power on the track.

"I saw him work this morning," Christina said. "I want to find out more about him. That is one outstanding racehorse."

"I wonder who he is," Melanie said, eyeing the massive colt.

"I can tell you." Cindy's voice made Christina turn. The Tall Oaks trainer had Gratis on a lead. Like Star, the bay colt was shiny from a recent bath, his head up and his ears pricked. He nickered when he saw Christina, who reached out to rub his glossy forehead.

"His name is Magnifique," Cindy said, gazing at the colt, who balked for a moment at the pull from the mechanical walker, then, with a toss of his head, continued walking in a steady circle.

"Where did he come from?" Christina asked.

"How come we haven't heard anything about him?"

"He was bred in Kentucky," Cindy said. "A friend of Ben's bought him at the Keeneland auction for twenty thousand dollars. Can you believe that horse sold for so little money?" She shook her head. "Maybe Ben and I will get that lucky this fall and find a colt like that."

"But he hasn't been racing in the United States," Christina said. "If his races had been anything like the way I saw him work this morning, the newspapers would have been all over him."

Cindy nodded. "He's been training in Saudi Arabia," she said. "It's too late for him to enter the Preakness, but the owner, Adel Abdullah, wants to run him in the Belmont." Cindy gazed at the handsome colt. "If I owned him, I'd sure race him."

Christina felt another weight settle on her shoulders. She knew the races were open to any horse qualified to compete, but she didn't want to see a horse that looked as though he could create a sonic boom racing against Star.

Gratis tossed his head and struck at the ground, tugging at the lead. Cindy gave the antsy colt a baleful look. "I need to go put him away," she said. "Beckie should be done cleaning his stall by now."

Cindy led her colt away, and Christina and Melanie

returned to Whitebrook's assigned stall. Dani was still in her chair, reading a textbook.

"Are you taking summer classes?" Christina asked, surprised. "I thought you were waiting until fall."

"I am waiting," Dani said, looking up. "But I need to take advanced chemistry next year, so I wanted to get a head start on the course." Dani planned to become a veterinarian. She had just completed her second year at the local community college and would be attending the University of Kentucky in the fall.

"Do you really like taking all those classes?" Christina asked. "It sounds like so much work."

"It is," Dani said firmly. "But it's worth the effort because I'll be able to help the animals I love."

Christina left Dani to her reading and wandered the shed rows, thinking about what Dani had said. She had decided not to go to college because she was doing what she loved, being a jockey. But as Cindy had pointed out, she needed to plan for a time when she might not be able to ride anymore. Even if she went to college, though, what would she study?

That evening in the motel room, Christina tried to watch television, but most of the local programming was focused on the Preakness, and she didn't want to get psyched out by what the reporters were saying about the race. Dani had offered to sleep at the track to keep an eye on Star, and Christina regretted that she had agreed. She could use the colt's companionship.

She thought about Dani studying and remembered her own schoolwork. But when she pulled her textbook from her suitcase and tried to read, her mind kept going back to Star and the upcoming race, and finally she put the schoolbooks aside. Once the race was over, she told herself, she'd study hard for her finals. But at the moment she couldn't focus on anything except Saturday's race.

When the phone rang, she snagged it from the hook.

"Hello?"

"Chris!" Parker said.

Christina sat up on the bed, delighted to hear his voice. "Are you going to be here Saturday?" she asked.

"I doubt I can make it up to Baltimore for the race," he said, sounding regretful. "But I wanted you to know I was thinking about you."

Christina felt disappointment settle over her, and she struggled to sound upbeat. "I'm sure you're really busy," she replied, but the gnawing emptiness she felt made her realize how much she missed Parker. Only she couldn't tell him that. He was busy pursuing his own dream and didn't need her making demands on his time. "I'm glad you're thinking about me, anyway," she said.

After they ended the call, Christina rolled onto her back and stared at the ceiling. What was she going to do once the Triple Crown was over? Star still had a racing career ahead of him, but in another year or two he'd be standing at stud at Whitebrook. Parker would still be in college and competing with his horses. She'd have new horses to work, but she needed something more.

She thought about Dani again, working with the horses and her goal of becoming a veterinarian, and Christina started to wonder if her decision not to attend college in the fall was a smart one.

10

ON FRIDAY MORNING CHRISTINA OVERSLEPT. SHE WAS horrified when she awoke and saw the travel alarm clock beside her bed. She threw on her clothes and hurried to the track. When she got to Star's stall, the colt was finishing his breakfast. He looked up from his hay net and nickered in greeting when she came into the stall.

"Good morning," she said, patting his sleek shoulder. "I hope you slept better than I did last night."

In response, Star tore another mouthful of hay from the net. Christina sighed. "If there is such a thing as reincarnation, I want to come back as my own horse," she said, folding her arms across her chest and leaning back against the stall wall. "You are spoiled beyond belief, and you don't have any worries, do you?"

Star eyed her as he crunched his hay. "No," she continued. "You let me do all the fretting, and you just do what your instincts tell you to do." She sighed. "So tomorrow, when centuries of breeding tell you to run like the wind, you'll do it. And it'll be up to me to give you some direction." She nodded thoughtfully. "I know you'll do your best, Star. And I promise you, I'll do mine."

When she left the stall, the aisle was filling with people. Grooms called to each other, laughing and talking as they wheeled loads of soiled bedding away from the stalls, led horses toward the back of the shed row for their baths, and prepared the horses scheduled for the day's races.

Melanie strolled up to the stall, smiling brightly. "Jazz called me this morning," she said cheerfully. "He can't be here for the race."

"You sound awfully happy about it," Christina replied, thinking of how she had felt when Parker told her he wouldn't be able to make it to watch the Preakness.

Melanie nodded, a dreamy expression on her face. "He told me he misses me the way the moon misses the sun's light," she said, heaving a gusty sigh. "Can you believe that? It's so romantic."

Christina thought about how she felt about Parker, and she nodded. "It sounds like a line from a song," she said. "A love song."

"It is," Melanie said. "He said he's writing it about me. Isn't that crazy?"

Christina glanced into Star's stall, then back at her cousin. "Yeah," she said slowly, wondering what it would be like to have someone write a love song about her. Parker would never do something like that.

"I'm heading over to Celtic Meadows' stalls," Melanie said. "Do you want to go along?"

"No, thanks," Christina said. "I'm going to hang out here with Star for a while." Melanie started to leave. "Mel," Christina said, and her cousin turned to look at her. "I'm really happy for you and Jazz," Christina said, smiling warmly.

Melanie blinked, then smiled back. "Thanks, Chris," she said. "I know things have been a little weird between us for the last few months, but you know, you're still one of the best people I know." She turned and hurried away, and Christina settled onto the chair in front of Star's stall and dug her school-books from her bag.

After reading through her world problems text one last time, she set the book aside and rose, stretching her neck and back. "It's going to be a long day," she told the colt. "I'll be glad when tomorrow is behind us, won't you?"

But Star merely shoved his nose at her, demanding a pet. Christina complied, rubbing the base of his ears gently. Star lowered his eyelids and cocked his head, making Christina laugh. "You have the same look on your face that Melanie had when she was talking about Jazz," she told the colt. "Are you madly in love with me?"

A group of people was strolling down the walkway, and Christina grimaced when she saw Brad and Lavinia Townsend in the center. When they neared, Brad cast a look in her direction. "Christina," he said, pulling his lips into a false smile. "How is your colt doing?"

"Star's fine," Christina replied, keeping her voice neutral.

Brad looked around at the people surrounding him. "This is the young woman who bought out my interest in Wonder's Star when the colt was deathly ill," he announced. "We were so pleased that Chris was able to bring Star around to the point of at least riding him again." He let his cool gaze linger on Christina's face. "It's just a shame he doesn't have that competitive edge that could have made him a real winner."

Christina felt her jaw drop, and she glared at Brad.

"Are you going to retire him to stud after the Belmont?" a man standing beside Brad asked.

Christina shot him a hard look. "I haven't made any decisions about retiring the colt," she said. "Star is in great shape and he's ready to race."

"But he isn't nearly the caliber of horse that Celtic Mist is," Brad said, speaking to the group. "He proved that in the Derby." Brad turned his attention back to Christina. "Unfortunately you're throwing a lot of money away trying to show that the colt has his mother's drive and courage." He shook his head. "I think that illness last winter took a lot more out of the horse than Whitebrook is willing to admit."

Christina gasped, angry words buzzing in her head. *He's just trying to psych you out*, she told herself, gritting her teeth before the words spilled across her lips. She forced herself to smile and took a deep breath. "I do wish you the best of luck tomorrow with Celtic Mist," she told Brad. "Celtic Meadows has some very well-bred horses, and you were so lucky to be able to buy a colt with such good bloodlines, since you couldn't produce one worthy of the Triple Crown at Townsend Acres."

To Christina's satisfaction, Lavinia's face went white and her eyes bulged, while Brad narrowed his eyes and glared at her. Just as quickly, he stretched another smile across his face, then turned to his entourage, gesturing for them to follow. "I do wish you luck tomorrow, Chris," he said in a cheerful tone. "You're going to need it."

As the group walked away, Christina sank onto her chair, shaking so badly, her knees knocked. She pressed her hands to her face and breathed deeply, trying to regain her composure.

"He's a pompous jerk."

Christina jumped, snapping her head up to see Ghyllian Hollis standing near Star's stall.

"You heard all that?" Christina asked.

"Every last word," Ghyllian said, winking at Christina. "You did good, facing down that weasel."

"Thanks," Christina said. "He just makes me so mad."

"I can understand why," Ghyllian said. "The reason I came by was to invite you and your family to a little party this evening."

Christina thought of the pre-Derby party she had attended at Townsend Acres, and she started to shake her head in refusal. She didn't want to dress up and do all the posturing that went along with attending social functions with the rich and famous. She just wanted to ride.

143

"I'm only having a select few people," Ghyllian said. "I don't go in much for the big show-off shindigs where the guest lists read like a who's who of the racing world." She offered Christina a warm smile. "I think you'd enjoy it."

"I'll check with my parents," Christina replied.

"Good," Ghyllian said. "But I won't take no for an answer. I'll see you tonight."

That evening when the Reeses arrived at the banquet room Ghyllian Hollis had rented for her party, Ben and Cindy greeted them at the door. "There's someone here we want you to meet," Cindy said, catching Ashleigh by the arm. She turned to a tall, dark-haired man standing by Ben. "This is Adel Abdullah," she said. "His colt, Magnifique, will be running in the Belmont."

"Please, call me Del," the man said, reaching out to shake Mike's hand, then Ashleigh's. "It is a pleasure to meet all of you." He turned to Christina and Melanie. "Especially these two talented young women." He smiled at Melanie. "Your filly, Perfect Image, is a remarkable racehorse. I was pleased to hear that she is recovering from the injury she sustained in the Derby."

"Image is a fighter," Melanie said proudly. "Her owner and I are just sorry she won't have the opportunity to compete in the other races."

144

Del nodded. "Her true test will be when her foals are on the track," he said. "We will see then if she passes her winning spirit on, much like Ashleigh's Wonder did to Star." He smiled at Christina. "I wish you only the best of luck tomorrow."

Christina immediately liked Del Abdullah. "Thank you," she said. "I'm looking forward to the competition. Star and I are both ready for the race."

Ashleigh nodded. "It's going to be exciting," she agreed.

As the adults slipped into a conversation about racing in Saudi Arabia, Christina saw Vince Jones across the room. When he gestured to her, she walked over to where he was talking with two jockeys Christina knew well. Tommy Turner and Vicky Frontiere had helped her get her jockey's license the previous spring.

Tommy gave her a quick hug. "I'm going to be racing against you and Star tomorrow," he informed her. "Vince and Ghyllian have asked me to ride Wild 'n' Free for Celtic Meadows."

"And we were lucky enough to have you agree," Vince said. "With you on board, the colt should make a good showing tomorrow."

Christina looked from Tommy to Vicky, wondering if she could outride two of the best jockeys she knew.

"I don't think you have to worry about a lot of pressure from my mount," Vicky said, rolling her eyes. "I think it's enough for TV Time that he made it into the race at all." She laughed. "Of course, I feel the same way about me. I consider it a privilege just to be riding in these races."

"Me too," Tommy said. "For all the years I've worked as a jockey, this is the first time I've been given a shot at one of the Triple Crown races."

After a few minutes, Christina walked away, wandering toward the long table covered with silver trays, each holding a variety of canapés. Even though she wasn't very hungry, Christina couldn't resist trying some of the different appetizers. She picked up a plate and eyed the food, trying to decide which items to sample.

"It all looks good, doesn't it?"

She looked across the table to see Steve Cauthen smiling at her. "I highly recommend the crab-stuffed mushrooms," he said. "Or the salmon pâté."

Taking his advice, Christina soon had a full plate. She found a chair and sat near the back wall, Steve at her side.

"This is delicious," she said, biting into a piece of cucumber spread with salmon pâté. "I'm glad I took your advice."

"Can I offer you a little more?" he asked. Steve

regarded her closely, leaning forward and resting his elbows on his knees.

Christina stopped chewing and looked at the Triple Crown-winning jockey. "Of course," she said, eager to hear what Steve had to say.

"You have a great horse under you, Chris," Steve told her. "You need to go onto the track feeling confident, even with a field full of tough horses to beat. Being sure of yourself and your horse is the biggest hurdle for you."

"I know," Christina said with a sigh. "But most of those jockeys have so much more experience than I have. I know Star is good, but I'm not the caliber of jockey that Tommy Turner is, or Emilio Casados, or Vicky Frontiere."

Steve smiled a little. "But you've been riding for years," he countered. "You've got experience—all you need is a little more confidence in your connection with your horse. Going out there knowing you've got a great horse under you is really important."

"Is that how you felt when you rode Affirmed in the Triple Crown races?" Christina asked.

Steve nodded. "I was only eighteen," he said. "Some jockeys ride all their lives and never get the chance to ride a great horse like Affirmed. I worked hard to get that far."

Christina nodded. "Getting up at five o'clock every morning, riding every horse you can get named on, studying race films, all of it. I know," she said.

"There's more," Steve said. "I was lucky enough to have people who believed in me, and a horse with the courage and strength to run a tough race." He cocked his head and looked directly at Christina. "A jockey's life is hours of agony for minutes of glory. But putting all that knowledge and hard work to good use is very satisfying. I did it with Affirmed, and I am sure you can do it with Star. The horse is willing, and from what I've seen, he does whatever you ask. It's rare to have that kind of bond with your horse. You're very lucky. Use it to your advantage, Chris. If you ride the best race you possibly can, you can pull it off tomorrow."

"Thank you," Christina said, trying to absorb the jockey's advice.

Steve rose. "I'll be cheering for you," he said.

"Thanks." Christina watched Steve walk away, her mind filled with what he had told her. Confidence was everything, she reminded herself. And the next day she and Star were going to ride the best race of their lives.

11

CHRISTINA STOOD WITH HER PARENTS IN THE VIEWING paddock, watching the colts being paraded in for the Preakness. TV Time had drawn the number one position. As the colt was led by, Christina eyed him closely. He looked good, but Christina knew he didn't have the staying power that the other horses in the field possessed. The next colt, Celtic Meadows' Wild 'n' Free, was wearing number two. When the handsome chestnut colt pranced by, Christina heard the fans crowded around the paddock start to murmur.

"He looks like Affirmed," she heard someone say.

"What a build."

"I'm going to go put some money on him to win."

Several people left the paddock, heading for the betting windows.

"He is exceptional," Ashleigh said quietly, glancing at Christina. "I think he's going to be the biggest threat to you today, Chris."

Christina sighed. "He doesn't look like a horse who likes to be beaten," she admitted. The colt had all the qualities of a top racehorse, with his powerful build and an eagle's sharpness in his alert expression. He had his head up and moved energetically. Besides that, he had an excellent starting position. With Tommy Turner riding him, the colt had a very good chance of winning the race.

The number three horse, Ingleside, walked past them, followed by Star. Christina tried to look at her colt as though she had never seen him before, sizing him up as though he were just one more racehorse. But everything in her told her that Star was the best horse in the field. His muscles rippled beneath his glossy chestnut coat, his head was up, and he pranced a little as Dani led him around the paddock, as if showing the crowd that he was the horse to watch in the race. Christina hoped that was true, but after his showing in the Derby, none of the fans seemed to see what she knew about her horse.

Gratis was in the number five slot. Christina was a

little concerned about him starting next to Star, not because she was afraid he would outrun her colt, but because she wasn't sure she trusted Wolf to ride a clean race. She felt butterflies start to flitter in her stomach and she pressed her palm against her midriff, trying to stop the nervous trembling. *We'll get clear of Wolf as soon as we hit the track,* she told herself. *I'm not going to let him try any of his little stunts on Star and me.*

Celtic Mist had the number six gate. The handsome gray colt was intimidating, and Christina knew he would be serious competition in the race. Brad and Lavinia stood with Emilio Casados, their jockey, and Christina thought of what Wolf had told her about the rider and his injured knee. But that didn't matter to her. Star would win because he was worthy, not because of another jockey's weakness.

Speed.com followed Celtic Mist, and Christina stared hard at the racehorse. He seemed to be favoring his right hind leg a little, but as he moved she wasn't sure if she was trying to see something wrong with the colt or if he really did have a little hitch in his gait.

War Ghost and Derry O'Dell had the eighth and ninth positions, and while Christina knew they didn't compare to Star, she knew better than to take either of the colts for granted.

When Dani brought Star around again, Christina

stepped forward and Mike gave her a boost onto the saddle. He patted her knee and offered her a nervous smile. "Good luck out there, honey," he said, stepping back as Dani led Star off. At the opening to the track, a group of pony riders on their retired racehorses and sturdy quarter horses waited for the mounts they would lead through the post parade. Star was handed off to a man on a big black gelding, and when they rode onto the track, the butterflies in Christina's stomach began a little stampede of their own. She forced herself to concentrate on Star, how he was moving, and how the track felt. The sunshine warmed the air, and a quick glance toward the grandstand showed it packed with fans who had turned out for the running of the Preakness.

When they were being loaded into the starting gate, Christina leaned forward and patted Star's sleek neck. "We're going to give them a great show, aren't we, boy?" she asked, settling onto the saddle as the gate crew shut them into their chute.

The air felt dense with pressure as Christina slipped her goggles into place and leaned forward over the colt's withers, tangling his mane in her fingers, bracing herself for the start. Star shifted his weight, eager to get onto the track and run. Around her, Christina heard the jingle of bits, the soft snorts of the tense Thoroughbreds, the quiet murmuring of the jockeys talking to their mounts, the squeaking of saddles, and the rustle of the jockeys' silks. It felt like an eternity before she heard the call "One back" and the last horse was loaded.

Christina swallowed and took a deep breath. "We're just going to go out and do it, boy," she told Star. The colt grunted and stamped his front feet impatiently.

"Hold on," she murmured, tightening her grip on the reins. The gate snapped open just as Star gave a little buck. As he propelled himself forward, Christina felt Star's front end buckle, and as they moved onto the track, his head and neck pitched forward. Christina saw the expanse of track, felt the terrible lurch as Star stumbled, and she pressed her fists into his shoulders, trying to keep from flying over his head and onto the track.

Around them, the other horses surged ahead. Christina choked back a scream as Star scrambled to keep his feet.

We're both going to get hurt, Christina thought wildly, knowing there was nothing she could do to save Star. She started to duck her head and pull her shoulder in, prepared to roll onto the track, when Star gave a tremendous leap into the air, pulling his feet back under him.

Before Christina had a chance to collect the reins again, the colt galloped frantically along the track, determined to catch the rest of the field. Christina fought to regain her own balance and froze in the saddle, trying to feel if Star's gait was off. If the colt had injured himself, she had to stop him before he did more damage.

But Star felt strong and steady beneath her. "We can still do this, boy!" she cried. "It's a long race and we can catch up!" She rose in the stirrups, elated with the colt's recovery. "Let's go!" She hunched over the colt's shoulders and urged him on.

Star dug in, stretching his legs so that he was covering several yards of the track with each stride. They drew close to the slower horses within a few seconds, and without thought, Christina took Star wide to get away from the traffic.

As they passed TV Time, Vicky glanced over at her and grinned. "Go, Chris," the other jockey called, still pushing her own colt to pick up his speed.

Gratis was closing in on Celtic Mist, Wild 'n' Free, and Speed.com. As they came into the first curve, Star's nose was nearly at Wolf's toe. Wolf darted a look under his arm, and Christina saw the surprise register on his face when he saw Star catching up with him. Wolf brought his whip down on Gratis's hip, urging

the bay colt to speed up. Gratis responded by lengthening his own strides, pulling ahead of Star by a few
feet, narrowing the gap between Gratis and the lead
horses.

Christina could hear Star's deep breaths and felt
the effort he was putting into each stride, but she could
tell the colt had a lot more to give. "Come on," she
begged him. "We have to make up for lost time, boy."
Star flicked his ears and laid them back, stretching his
neck out and pumping his legs even harder.

Gratis was near Celtic Mist, and Christina saw
Wolf push the colt toward a tiny gap between the
Townsend horse and Speed.com. *Aggressive riding,* she
thought, balancing as lightly as she could over Star's
shoulders. "Can you give me more, Star?" she asked
the colt, kneading her hands along his neck. Star
strained to run even faster as they moved to the
straight, catching up with the four horses leading the
race.

On the inside rail, Wild 'n' Free was in the clear,
Tommy riding skillfully, keeping his colt in a good
position. Beside him, Celtic Mist looked strong and
steady. Christina remembered Wolf talking about
Emilio's bad knee, but she had her hands full with Star.
If Wolf did something illegal, the track officials would
be the ones to deal with him. She needed to focus on

getting Star into a winning position after his disastrous start.

They rode through the turn, and Wolf brought his whip down on Gratis's hip again. The colt dove forward, cutting in front of Star to squeeze in between Celtic Mist and Speed.com.

As Gratis moved in front of them, Star faltered and went wide. Before Christina could help him recover, Wild 'n' Free, Celtic Mist, and Gratis were several strides ahead. Star dug in, flying past Speed.com in a valiant effort to catch the three lead horses.

But Christina knew the effort was costing her colt, and she didn't push him, her concern more on Star's well-being than making up track. Star fought her, trying to move out, and they crossed the finish line in fourth place, almost neck and neck with Gratis and just a few strides ahead of Speed.com. And as Christina slowed Star, she patted his neck, proud of the effort he had put into the race. "We may not have won," she told the colt, "but you showed everyone that you have the courage to do your best in spite of everything."

Ashleigh, Dani, and Ian met her on the track, all of them concerned with the stress the race had put on Star's legs. "We'll have the vet check him over completely," Ian said, running his hands down the colt's front legs. He looked up at Christina. "That was some great riding you did," he told her.

Christina smiled, patting Star's shoulder. "Star did it all," she said.

As Ian and Dani led Star off the track, Ashleigh gave Christina a hug. "You did a terrific job," she said.

Christina gave her mother a wide-eyed look. "But we didn't even show," she protested. "Cindy and Ben should be happy that Gratis placed third again."

Ashleigh shook her head. "Wolf got disqualified," she said. "That means Star got third place."

Christina's mouth dropped open. She was sorry to hear that Wolf's riding had cost Ben and Cindy their showing in the race. But as she headed along the outside rail, Cindy waved her over. Ben stood beside her, and next to them were Samantha and Tor Nelson and Melanie, who gave her a tight hug when she got to the rail.

"You guys did great," Melanie said. "I'm so proud of you both."

"Thanks, Mel," Christina said.

"I'm sorry about my jockey," Cindy said, shaking her head in disgust. "I think Star could have pulled it off, Chris. If it hadn't been for Wolf's little stunt, I truly believe Star could have won the Preakness."

Christina gaped at her, but Ben nodded in agreement. "Next is the Belmont," he said. "We'll have a different jockey for Gratis, so we're not giving anything away, but your horse was truly amazing."

"I have to agree, you did some excellent riding," she heard a familiar voice say. She turned to see Steve Cauthen smiling at her from the rail. "I'm looking forward to seeing you at Belmont."

Christina thanked everyone and hurried to the vet barn, where she saw Ian and Dani standing outside Star's stall.

"He's fine," Ian said happily. "No damage, but we need to rest him well and keep those legs wrapped."

Christina slipped inside the stall and wrapped her arms around Star's neck. "We've got one more chance," she said, giving him a hug. "In two more weeks we'll be at Belmont, and you'll get to try again. But no matter what happens," she said, looking into the colt's keen eyes, "I know that you are the greatest horse in the world, and I'm the luckiest person I know."

Joe Ithier riding Affirmed   ©1978 Bettman/Corbis

AFFIRMED

February 21, 1975–January 12, 2001

The 1978 Triple Crown winner, Affirmed, was born February 21, 1975, at Harbor View Farm in Florida. Trained by Lazaro Barrera and ridden by jockey Steve Cauthen, the chestnut Thoroughbred raced twenty-nine times, winning twenty-two races, with five seconds and only one third, racing under Harbor View Farms' flamingo-pink-and-black silks. Affirmed beat Alydar, his top rival, by just a nose in the 1978 Kentucky Derby. Affirmed was laid to rest at Jonabell Farms in Lexington, Kentucky, on January 12, 2001.

Mary Newhall Anderson spent her childhood exploring back roads and trails on horseback with her best friend. She now lives with her family and horses on Washington State's Olympic Peninsula. Mary has written novels and short stories for both adults and young adults.

WIN A FREE RIDING SADDLE!

ENTER THE
THOROUGHBRED RIDING SADDLE
SWEEPSTAKES!

COMPLETE THIS ENTRY FORM • NO PURCHASE NECESSARY

NAME: _____

ADDRESS: _____   _____

CITY: _____ STATE: _____ ZIP: _____

PHONE: _____ AGE: _____

MAIL TO: THOROUGHBRED RIDING SADDLE SWEEPSTAKES!
c/o HarperCollins, Attn.: Department AW
10 E. 53rd Street   New York, NY 10022

HarperEntertainment

17th Street Productions,
an Alloy Online, Inc., company

THOROUGHBRED 58 SWEEPSTAKES RULES

——————— OFFICIAL RULES ———————

1. No purchase necessary.

2. To enter, complete the official entry form or hand print your name, address, and phone number along with the words "Thoroughbred Riding Saddle Sweepstakes" on a 3" x 5" card and mail to: HarperCollins, Attn.: Department AW, 10 E. 53rd Street, New York, NY 10022. Entries must be received by October 1, 2003. Enter as often as you wish, but each entry must be mailed separately. One entry per envelope. Partially completed, illegible, or mechanically reproduced entries will not be accepted. Sponsors are not responsible for lost, late, mutilated, illegible, stolen, postage due, incomplete, or misdirected entries. All entries become the property of HarperCollins and will not be returned.

3. Sweepstakes open to all legal residents of the United States (excluding residents of Colorado and Rhode Island) who are between the ages of eight and

sixteen by October 1, 2003, excluding employees and immediate family members of HarperCollins, Alloy, Inc., or 17th Street Productions, an Alloy company, and their respective subsidiaries, and affiliates, officers, directors, shareholders, employees, agents, attorneys, and other representatives (individually and collectively), and their respective parent companies, affiliates, subsidiaries, advertising, promotion and fulfillments agencies, and the persons with whom each of the above are domiciled. Offer void where prohibited or restricted.

4. Odds of winning depend on total number of entries received. Approximately 100,000 entry forms distributed. All prizes will be awarded. Winners will be randomly drawn on or about October 15, 2003, by representatives of Harper-Collins, whose decisions are final. Potential winners will be notified by mail and a parent or guardian of the potential winner will be required to sign and return an affadavit of eligibility and release of liability within 14 days of notification. Failure to return affadavit within the specified time period will disqualify winner and another winner will be chosen. By acceptance of prize, winner consents to the use of his or her name, photographs, likeness, and personal information by HarperCollins, Alloy, Inc., and 17th Street Productions, an Alloy company, for publicity and advertising purposes without further compensation except where prohibited.

5. One (1) Grand Prize Winner will receive a Thoroughbred riding saddle. HarperCollins reserves the right at its sole discretion to substitute another prize of equal or of greater value in the event prize is unavailable. Approximate retail value $500.00.

6. Only one prize will be awarded per individual, family, or household. Prizes are nontransferable and cannot be sold or redeemed for cash. No cash substitute is available except at the sole discretion of HarperCollins for reasons of prize unavailability. Any federal, state, or local taxes are the responsibility of the winner.

7. Additional terms: By participating, entrants agree a) to the official rules and decisions of the judges which will be final in all respects; and b) to release, discharge, and hold harmless HarperCollins, Alloy Online, Inc., and 17th Street Productions, an Alloy Online, Inc., company, and their affiliates, subsidiaries, and advertising promotion agencies from and against any and all liability or damages associated with acceptance, use, or misuse of any prize received in this sweepstakes.

8. To obtain the name of the winner, please send your request and a self-addressed stamped envelope (Vermont residents may omit return postage) to "Thoroughbred Riding Saddle Winners List," c/o HarperCollins, Attn.: Department AW, 10 E. 53rd Street, New York, NY 10022.

SPONSOR: HarperCollins*Publishers* Inc.